DOVER·THRIFT·EDITIONS

Henry IV, Part I

WILLIAM SHAKESPEARE

DOVER PUBLICATIONS, INC.
Mineola, New York

DOVER THRIFT EDITIONS

GENERAL EDITOR: STANLEY APPELBAUM
EDITOR OF THIS VOLUME: ADAM FROST

Theatrical Rights

This Dover Thrift Edition may be used in its entirety, in adaptation or in any other way for theatrical productions, professional and amateur, in the United States, without fee, permission or acknowledgment. (This may not apply outside the United States, as copyright conditions may vary.)

Copyright

Published in Canada by General Publishing Company, Ltd., 30 Lesmill Road, Don Mills, Toronto, Ontario.
Published in the United Kingdom by Constable and Company, Ltd., 3 The Lanchesters, 162–164 Fulham Palace Road, London W6 9ER.

Bibliographical Note

This Dover edition, first published in 1997, contains the unabridged text of *The First Part of King Henry IV* as published in Volume XII of *The Caxton Edition of the Complete Works of William Shakespeare*, Caxton Publishing Company, London, n.d. The Note was prepared specially for this edition, and explanatory footnotes from the Caxton edition have been supplemented and revised.

Library of Congress Cataloging-in-Publication Data

Shakespeare, William, 1564–1616.
   [King Henry. Part 1]
   Henry IV, Part I / William Shakespeare.
      p.   cm. — (Dover thrift editions)
   "... contains the unabridged text of The first part of King Henry IV as published in volume XII of The Caxton edition of the complete works of William Shakespeare, Caxton Publishing Company, London, n.d." — T.p. verso.
   ISBN 0-486-29584-2 (pbk.)
    1. Henry IV, King of England, 1367–1413 — Drama.   2. Great Britain — Kings and rulers — Drama.   I. Title.   II. Series.
PR2810.A1   1997
822.3'3 — dc20
                                             96-39012
                                               CIP

Manufactured in the United States of America
Dover Publications, Inc., 31 East 2nd Street, Mineola, N.Y. 11501

Note

HENRY IV, PART I (c. 1596–1597) follows closely upon the action of Shakespeare's *Richard II*, which ended with Henry Bolingbroke newly crowned as the King of England. Echoing the conclusion of that play, *1 Henry IV* opens with the king planning to undertake a crusade to the Holy Land, in part to assuage his guilt over the death of his predecessor and in part to unify his countrymen now that civil strife within England has seemingly come to an end. His plans are soon shattered, however, by the news of rebellion in Wales and in Scotland, and of the disobedience of his former ally Henry Spencer (called Hotspur). The play thus begins with conflict, and conflict marks it throughout, from Hotspur's early defiance of the king's orders, to the split between the king and his old supporters, to the battle at Shrewsbury with which the action closes.

Besides being a portrait of a nation's unrest, *1 Henry IV* is a study in contrasts. Sir John Falstaff, for instance, comic and vice-ridden, acts as a foil to the careworn King Henry: the men compete as father-figures to Harry, Prince of Wales, the one leading him toward vice and folly, the other demanding the prince uphold the responsibilities of his position. The dissolute prince himself has his opposite in the other Harry, the impetuous Hotspur. It is King Henry's regret that the one is his son and not the other, for in Hotspur he finds conduct becoming of a prince, while "riot and dishonour stain the brow / Of my young Harry." The prince is not blind to his father's preference, and all along he plans to redeem his father's favor by reforming, even while reveling in the company of Falstaff; by mending his ways, he thinks, he will stand in marked contrast to his former self and win more acclaim than would have been his had he played the dutiful prince from the start. That his reformation will require him to cast off Falstaff is an unfortunate necessity; that it leads to the killing of his rival Hotspur is inevitable.

As he had for many of his history plays, Shakespeare used Raphael Holinshed's *Chronicles of England, Scotland and Ireland* (1587) as the principal source of the historical material in *1 Henry IV*, and some of Holinshed's factual errors have been carried over into this play. The anonymous play *The Famous Victories of Henry V* may have provided Shakespeare with the details of the young prince's dissipated behavior, although the theme had long been a part of popular tradition. Probably composed soon after *The Merchant of Venice*, *1 Henry IV* was first entered in the Stationers' Register on February 25th, 1598, and was printed later that year. It has since proved to be one of Shakespeare's most popular plays, and Sir John Falstaff has become one of his best-loved creations.

Contents

Dramatis Personae

KING HENRY the Fourth.
HENRY, Prince of Wales, } sons to the King.
JOHN of Lancaster,
EARL OF WESTMORELAND.
SIR WALTER BLUNT.
THOMAS PERCY, Earl of Worcester.
HENRY PERCY, Earl of Northumberland.
HENRY PERCY, surnamed HOTSPUR, his son.
EDMUND MORTIMER, Earl of March.
RICHARD SCROOP, Archbishop of York.
ARCHIBALD, Earl of DOUGLAS.
OWEN GLENDOWER.
SIR RICHARD VERNON.
SIR JOHN FALSTAFF.
SIR MICHAEL, a friend to the Archbishop of York.
POINS.
GADSHILL.
PETO.
BARDOLPH.

LADY PERCY, wife to Hotspur, and sister to Mortimer.
LADY MORTIMER, daughter to Glendower, and wife to Mortimer.
MISTRESS QUICKLY, hostess of a tavern in Eastcheap.

Lords, Officers, Sheriff, Vintner, Chamberlain, Drawers, two
Carriers, Travellers, and Attendants

SCENE: *England and Wales*

ACT I.

SCENE I. *London. The Palace.*

Enter KING HENRY, LORD JOHN of LANCASTER, the EARL of
WESTMORELAND, SIR WALTER BLUNT, *and others*

KING. So shaken as we are, so wan with care,
Find we a time for frighted peace to pant,
And breathe short-winded accents of new broils
To be commenced in stronds afar remote.[1]
No more the thirsty entrance of this soil
Shall daub her lips with her own children's blood;
No more shall trenching war channel her fields,
Nor bruise her flowerets with the armed hoofs
Of hostile paces: those opposed[2] eyes,
Which, like the meteors of a troubled heaven,
All of one nature, of one substance bred,
Did lately meet in the intestine[3] shock
And furious close[4] of civil butchery,
Shall now, in mutual well-beseeming[5] ranks,
March all one way, and be no more opposed
Against acquaintance, kindred and allies:
The edge of war, like an ill-sheathed knife,
No more shall cut his master. Therefore, friends,
As far as to the sepulchre of Christ,
Whose soldier now, under whose blessed cross
We are impressed and engaged to fight,
Forthwith a power of English shall we levy;
Whose arms were moulded in their mothers' womb
To chase these pagans in those holy fields
Over whose acres walk'd those blessed feet,

---

1. *Find we . . . remote*] Let us allow domestic peace time to recover breath, and speak briefly
   of new campaigns to be waged on foreign shores.
2. *opposed*] hostile.
3. *intestine*] domestic, coming to pass between people of the same nation.
4. *close*] hand-to-hand grapple.
5. *mutual well-beseeming*] united (by common sentiment) and fitly equipped.

1

Which fourteen hundred years ago were nail'd
For our advantage on the bitter cross.
But this our purpose now is twelve month old,
And bootless 'tis to tell you we will go:
Therefore we meet not now.[6] Then let me hear
Of you, my gentle cousin Westmoreland,
What yesternight our council did decree
In forwarding this dear expedience.[7]

WEST.   My liege, this haste was hot in question,
And many limits of the charge[8] set down
But yesternight: when all athwart there came
A post from Wales loaden with heavy news;
Whose worst was, that the noble Mortimer,
Leading the men of Herefordshire to fight
Against the irregular and wild Glendower,
Was by the rude hands of that Welshman taken,
A thousand of his people butchered;
Upon whose dead corpse[9] there was such misuse,
Such beastly shameless transformation,
By those Welshwomen done, as may not be
Without much shame retold or spoken of.

KING.   It seems then that the tidings of this broil
Brake off our business for the Holy Land.

WEST.   This match'd with other did, my gracious lord;
For more uneven[10] and unwelcome news
Came from the north and thus it did import:
On Holy-rood day,[11] the gallant Hotspur there,
Young Harry Percy, and brave Archibald,[12]
That ever-valiant and approved Scot,
At Holmedon met,
Where they did spend a sad and bloody hour;
As by discharge of their artillery,
And shape of likelihood, the news was told;
For he that brought them, in the very heat
And pride of their contention did take horse,
Uncertain of the issue any way.

KING.   Here is a dear, a true industrious friend,

---

6. *Therefore we meet not now*] This is not the object of our present meeting.
7. *this dear expedience*] this important expedition.
8. *limits of the charge*] definite arrangements of the undertaking.
9. *corpse*] used for the plural "corpses."
10. *more uneven*] more troublesome.
11. *Holy-rood day*] September 14.
12. *brave Archibald*] Archibald Douglas, the fourth Earl of Douglas.

Sir Walter Blunt, new lighted from his horse,
Stain'd with the variation of each soil
Betwixt that Holmedon and this seat of ours;
And he hath brought us smooth and welcome news.
The Earl of Douglas is discomfited:
Ten thousand bold Scots, two and twenty knights,
Balk'd[13] in their own blood did Sir Walter see
On Holmedon's plains. Of prisoners, Hotspur took
Mordake the Earl of Fife, and eldest son
To beaten Douglas;[14] and the Earl of Athol,
Of Murray, Angus, and Menteith:
And is not this an honourable spoil?
A gallant prize? ha, cousin, is it not?

WEST.   In faith,
It is a conquest for a prince to boast of.

KING.   Yea, there thou makest me sad and makest me sin
In envy that my Lord Northumberland
Should be the father to so blest a son,
A son who is the theme of honour's tongue;
Amongst a grove, the very straightest plant;
Who is sweet Fortune's minion[15] and her pride:
Whilst I, by looking on the praise of him,
See riot and dishonour stain the brow
Of my young Harry. O that it could be proved
That some night-tripping fairy had exchanged
In cradle-clothes our children where they lay,
And call'd mine Percy, his Plantagenet!
Then would I have his Harry, and he mine.
But let him from my thoughts. What think you, coz,[16]
Of this young Percy's pride? the prisoners,
Which he in this adventure hath surprised,
To his own use he keeps; and sends me word,
I shall have none but Mordake Earl of Fife.

WEST.   This is his uncle's teaching; this is Worcester,
Malevolent to you in all aspects;
Which makes him prune[17] himself, and bristle up
The crest of youth against your dignity.

KING.   But I have sent for him to answer this;

---

13. *Balk'd*] Heaped up.
14. *Mordake . . . Douglas*] Murdoch, Earl of Fife, was not in fact related to Douglas. He was
   also the Earl of Menteith mentioned in the following line.
15. *minion*] favorite.
16. *coz*] cousin, kinsman.
17. *prune*] preen.

And for this cause awhile we must neglect
Our holy purpose to Jerusalem.
Cousin, on Wednesday next our council we
Will hold at Windsor; so inform the lords:
But come yourself with speed to us again;
For more is to be said and to be done
Than out of anger can be uttered.
WEST. I will, my liege.   [*Exeunt.*

SCENE II. *London. An Apartment of the Prince's.*

Enter the PRINCE OF WALES *and* FALSTAFF

FAL. Now, Hal, what time of day is it, lad?

PRINCE. Thou art so fat-witted,[1] with drinking of old sack[2] and unbuttoning thee after supper and sleeping upon benches after noon, that thou hast forgotten to demand that truly which thou wouldst truly know. What a devil hast thou to do with the time of the day? Unless hours were cups of sack, and minutes capons, and clocks the tongues of bawds, and dials the signs of leaping-houses,[3] and the blessed sun himself a fair hot wench in flame-coloured taffeta, I see no reason why thou shouldst be so superfluous to demand the time of the day.

FAL. Indeed, you come near me now, Hal; for we that take purses go by the moon and the seven stars,[4] and not by Phœbus,[5] he, "that wandering knight so fair." And, I prithee, sweet wag, when thou art king, as, God save thy grace, — majesty I should say, for grace thou wilt have none, —

PRINCE. What, none?

FAL. No, by my troth, not so much as will serve to be prologue to an egg and butter.

PRINCE. Well, how then? come, roundly, roundly.[6]

1. *fat-witted*] dull-witted.
2. *sack*] a dry Spanish wine.
3. *leaping-houses*] brothels.
4. *the seven stars*] the Pleiades.
5. *Phœbus*] the sun.
6. *roundly*] directly, without evasion.

FAL. Marry, then, sweet wag, when thou art king, let not us that are
squires of the night's body be called thieves of the day's beauty:[7]
let us be Diana's foresters,[8] gentlemen of the shade, minions of the
moon; and let men say we be men of good government,[9] being
governed, as the sea is, by our noble and chaste mistress the moon,
under whose countenance we steal.

PRINCE. Thou sayest well, and it holds well too; for the fortune of us that
are the moon's men doth ebb and flow like the sea, being governed,
as the sea is, by the moon. As, for proof, now: a purse of gold most
resolutely snatched on Monday night and most dissolutely spent
on Tuesday morning; got with swearing "Lay by"[10] and spent with
crying "Bring in;"[11] now in as low an ebb as the foot of the ladder,
and by and by in as high a flow as the ridge of the gallows.

FAL. By the Lord, thou sayest true, lad. And is not my hostess of the
tavern a most sweet wench?

PRINCE. As the honey of Hybla,[12] my old lad of the castle.[13] And is not
a buff jerkin a most sweet robe of durance?[14]

FAL. How now, how now, mad wag! what, in thy quips and thy
quiddities?[15] what a plague have I to do with a buff jerkin?

PRINCE. Why, what a pox have I to do with my hostess of the tavern?

FAL. Well, thou hast called her to a reckoning many a time and oft.

PRINCE. Did I ever call for thee to pay thy part?

FAL. No; I'll give thee thy due, thou hast paid all there.

PRINCE. Yea, and elsewhere, so far as my coin would stretch; and where
it would not, I have used my credit.

FAL. Yea, and so used it that, were it not here apparent that thou art heir
apparent — But, I prithee, sweet wag, shall there be gallows standing in England when thou art king? and resolution thus fobbed[16]
as it is with the rusty curb of old father antic[17] the law? Do not thou,
when thou art king, hang a thief.

---

7. *let not us . . . day's beauty*] The general sense is that we who ply a (dishonest) trade by
night have no wish to be called thieves in daytime.
8. *Diana's foresters*] Diana was goddess both of the moon and of the chase.
9. *good government*] good conduct.
10. *"Lay by"*] The meaning is here "Stand close," the highwaymen's word to prepare for
attack on a passer-by.
11. *"Bring in"*] sc. drink.
12. *Hybla*] A town in Sicily celebrated for the sweetness of its honey.
13. *my old lad of the castle*] a punning allusion to the name of Sir John Oldcastle, which
Shakespeare bestowed on Falstaff in the first draft of the piece.
14. *a buff jerkin . . . durance*] Sheriff's officers were dressed in buff, and "durance" means
both "imprisonment" and a coarse cloth well known for its durability.
15. *quiddities*] quibbles.
16. *resolution thus fobbed*] boldness or courage thus foiled or deluded.
17. *antic*] buffoon.

PRINCE. No; thou shalt.

FAL. Shall I? O rare! By the Lord, I'll be a brave judge.

PRINCE. Thou judgest false already: I mean, thou shalt have the hanging of the thieves and so become a rare hangman.

FAL. Well, Hal, well; and in some sort it jumps with my humour as well as waiting in the court, I can tell you.

PRINCE. For obtaining of suits?

FAL. Yea, for obtaining of suits, whereof the hangman hath no lean wardrobe.[18] 'Sblood, I am as melancholy as a gib cat or a lugged bear.[19]

PRINCE. Or an old lion, or a lover's lute.

FAL. Yea, or the drone of a Lincolnshire bagpipe.

PRINCE. What sayest thou to a hare,[20] or the melancholy of Moorditch?[21]

FAL. Thou hast the most unsavoury similes, and art indeed the most comparative,[22] rascalliest, sweet young prince. But, Hal, I prithee, trouble me no more with vanity. I would to God thou and I knew where a commodity of good names were to be bought. An old lord of the council rated me the other day in the street about you, sir, but I marked him not; and yet he talked very wisely, but I regarded him not; and yet he talked wisely, and in the street too.

PRINCE. Thou didst well; for wisdom cries out in the streets, and no man regards it.[23]

FAL. O, thou hast damnable iteration,[24] and art indeed able to corrupt a saint. Thou hast done much harm upon me, Hal; God forgive thee for it! Before I knew thee, Hal, I knew nothing; and now am I, if a man should speak truly, little better than one of the wicked. I must give over this life, and I will give it over: by the Lord, an I do not, I am a villain: I'll be damned for never a king's son in Christendom.

PRINCE. Where shall we take a purse to-morrow, Jack?

FAL. 'Zounds, where thou wilt, lad; I'll make one; an I do not, call me villain and baffle[25] me.

PRINCE. I see a good amendment of life in thee; from praying to purse-taking.

---

18. *wardrobe*] The apparel of executed persons was the hangman's perquisite.
19. *gib cat . . . lugged bear*] a tomcat or a showman's chained bear.
20. *a hare*] The hare was credited by Elizabethans with a melancholy temperament.
21. *Moor-ditch*] A section of Finsbury which had a reputation for generating a very depressing climate. For Finsbury in general, see note 29 to Scene I of Act III.
22. *comparative*] fond of comparisons.
23. *wisdom . . . regards it*] Cf. *Proverbs*, 1:20, 24.
24. *damnable iteration*] an exasperating habit of repeating my words.
25. *baffle*] disgrace, degrade.

FAL. Why, Hal, 'tis my vocation. Hal; 'tis no sin for a man to labour in his vocation.

Enter POINS

Poins! Now shall we know if Gadshill have set a match.[26] O, if men were to be saved by merit, what hole in hell were hot enough for him? This is the most omnipotent villain that ever cried "Stand" to a true man.

PRINCE. Good morrow, Ned.

POINS. Good morrow, sweet Hal. What says Monsieur Remorse? what says Sir John Sack and Sugar?[27] Jack! how agrees the devil and thee about thy soul, that thou soldest him on Good Friday last for a cup of Madeira and a cold capon's leg?

PRINCE. Sir John stands to his word, the devil shall have his bargain; for he was never yet a breaker of proverbs: he will give the devil his due.

POINS. Then art thou damned for keeping thy word with the devil.

PRINCE. Else he had been damned for cozening the devil.

POINS. But, my lads, my lads, to-morrow morning, by four o'clock, early at Gadshill! there are pilgrims going to Canterbury with rich offerings, and traders riding to London with fat purses: I have vizards[28] for you all; you have horses for yourselves: Gadshill lies to-night in Rochester: I have bespoke supper to-morrow night in Eastcheap: we may do it as secure as sleep. If you will go, I will stuff your purses full of crowns; if you will not, tarry at home and be hanged.

FAL. Hear ye, Yedward;[29] if I tarry at home and go not, I'll hang you for going.

POINS. You will, chops?[30]

FAL. Hal, wilt thou make one?

PRINCE. Who, I rob? I a thief? not I, by my faith.

FAL. There's neither honesty, manhood, nor good fellowship in thee, nor thou camest not of the blood royal, if thou darest not stand for ten shillings.

PRINCE. Well then, once in my days I'll be a madcap.

FAL. Why, that's well said.

PRINCE. Well, come what will, I'll tarry at home.

FAL. By the Lord, I'll be a traitor then, when thou art king.

PRINCE. I care not.

POINS. Sir John, I prithee, leave the prince and me alone: I will lay him down such reasons for this adventure that he shall go.

---

26. *set a match*] made an appointment for nefarious purposes.
27. *Sack and Sugar*] It was the habit of Elizabethan topers to mix sugar with their wine.
28. *vizards*] masks.
29. *Yedward*] A colloquial form of Edward.
30. *chops*] flesh meat, "fat chops."

FAL. Well, God give thee the spirit of persuasion and him the ears of profiting, that what thou speakest may move and what he hears may be believed, that the true prince may, for recreation sake, prove a false thief; for the poor abuses of the time want countenance. Farewell: you shall find me in Eastcheap.

PRINCE. Farewell, thou latter spring! farewell, All-hallown summer![31]

[*Exit Falstaff.*

POINS. Now, my good sweet honey lord, ride with us to-morrow: I have a jest to execute that I cannot manage alone. Falstaff, Bardolph, Peto and Gadshill shall rob those men that we have already waylaid; yourself and I will not be there; and when they have the booty, if you and I do not rob them, cut this head off from my shoulders.

PRINCE. How shall we part with them in setting forth?

POINS. Why, we will set forth before or after them, and appoint them a place of meeting, wherein it is at our pleasure to fail, and then will they adventure upon the exploit themselves; which they shall have no sooner achieved, but we'll set upon them.

PRINCE. Yea, but 'tis like that they will know us by our horses, by our habits, and by every other appointment,[32] to be ourselves.

POINS. Tut! our horses they shall not see; I'll tie them in the wood; our vizards we will change after we leave them: and, sirrah, I have cases[33] of buckram for the nonce, to immask our noted outward garments.

PRINCE. Yea, but I doubt they will be too hard for us.

POINS. Well, for two of them, I know them to be as true-bred cowards as ever turned back; and for the third, if he fight longer than he sees reason, I'll forswear arms. The virtue of this jest will be, the incomprehensible lies that this same fat rogue will tell us when we meet at supper: how thirty, at least, he fought with; what wards,[34] what blows, what extremities he endured; and in the reproof[35] of this lies the jest.

PRINCE. Well, I'll go with thee: provide us all things necessary and meet me to-morrow night in Eastcheap; there I'll sup. Farewell.

POINS. Farewell, my lord. [*Exit.*

PRINCE. I know you all, and will a while uphold
The unyoked[36] humour of your idleness:
Yet herein will I imitate the sun, (s on ?)

---

31. *All-hallown summer*] Falstaff's summer (youth) has lasted to All-hallows Day, November 1.
32. *appointment*] equipment.
33. *cases*] overcoats.
34. *wards*] guards.
35. *reproof*] refutation.
36. *unyoked*] untamed, undisciplined, licentious.

Who doth permit the base contagious clouds
To smother up his beauty from the world,
That, when he please again to be himself,
Being wanted, he may be more wonder'd at,
By breaking through the foul and ugly mists
Of vapours that did seem to strangle him.
If all the year were playing holidays,
To sport would be as tedious as to work;
But when they seldom come they wish'd for come,
And nothing pleaseth but rare accidents.
So, when this loose behavior I throw off
And pay the debt I never promised,
By how much better than my word I am,
By so much shall I falsify men's hopes;
And like bright metal on a sullen ground,
My reformation, glittering o'er my fault,
Shall show more goodly and attract more eyes
Than that which hath no foil to set it off.
I'll so offend, to make offence a skill;[37]
Redeeming time when men think least I will.   [*Exit.*

*contrast
bad prince
to good king

couplet*

SCENE III. *London. The Palace.*

Enter the KING, NORTHUMBERLAND, WORCESTER, HOTSPUR,
SIR WALTER BLUNT, *with others*

KING.   My blood hath been too cold and temperate,
        Unapt to stir at these indignities,
        And you have found me;[1] for accordingly
        You tread upon my patience: but be sure
        I will from henceforth rather be myself,
        Mighty and to be fear'd, than my condition;[2]
        Which hath been smooth as oil, soft as young down,
        And therefore lost that title of respect
        Which the proud soul ne'er pays but to the proud.

_____

37. *to make offence a skill*] so as to derive advantage from obnoxious conduct.

_____

1. *found me*] found me out, *i.e.*, discovered my easy-going tendency.
2. *I will . . . my condition*] I will choose from now on to act the king, mighty and to be feared, than follow my natural temper.

WOR.   Our house, my sovereign liege, little deserves
The scourge of greatness to be used on it;
And that same greatness to which our own hands
Have holp to make so portly.

NORTH.   My lord, —

KING.   Worcester, get thee gone; for I do see
Danger and disobedience in thine eye:
O, sir, your presence is too bold and peremptory,
And majesty might never yet endure
The moody frontier[3] of a servant brow.
You have good leave[4] to leave us: when we need
Your use and counsel, we shall send for you.   [*Exit Wor.*
You were about to speak.   [*To North.*

NORTH.   Yea, my good lord.
Those prisoners in your highness' name demanded,
Which Harry Percy here at Holmedon took,
Were, as he says, not with such strength denied
As is deliver'd[5] to your majesty:
Either envy, therefore, or misprision[6]
Is guilty of this fault and not my son.

HOT.   My liege, I did deny no prisoners.
But I remember, when the fight was done,
When I was dry with rage and extreme toil,
Breathless and faint, leaning upon my sword,
Came there a certain lord, neat, and trimly dress'd,
Fresh as a bridegroom; and his chin new reap'd[7]
Show'd like a stubble-land at harvest-home;
He was perfumed like a milliner;[8]
And 'twixt his finger and his thumb he held
A pouncet-box,[9] which ever and anon
He gave his nose and took 't away again;
Who therewith angry, when it next came there,
Took it in snuff;[10] and still he smiled and talk'd,
And as the soldiers bore dead bodies by,
He call'd them untaught knaves, unmannerly,

---

3. *frontier*] front or forehead.
4. *good leave*] our full assent.
5. *deliver'd*] portrayed.
6. *envy . . . misprision*] malice . . . misunderstanding.
7. *chin new reap'd*] freshly trimmed, cropped close in accord with the fashionable vogue.
8. *milliner*] dealer in fancy articles of attire.
9. *A pouncet-box*] A box containing aromatic herbs, with a perforated cover.
10. *Took it in snuff*] Snuffed it up. The phrase, which also meant "took offence," has a double meaning here.

To bring a slovenly unhandsome corse
Betwixt the wind and his nobility.
With many holiday and lady terms
He question'd me; amongst the rest, demanded
My prisoners in your majesty's behalf.
I then, all smarting with my wounds being cold,
To be so pester'd with a popinjay,
Out of my grief[11] and my impatience,
Answer'd neglectingly I know not what,
He should, or he should not; for he made me mad
To see him shine so brisk, and smell so sweet,
And talk so like a waiting-gentlewoman
Of guns and drums and wounds, — God save the mark! —
And telling me the sovereign'st thing on earth
Was parmaceti[12] for an inward bruise;
And that it was great pity, so it was,
This villanous salt-petre should be digg'd
Out of the bowels of the harmless earth,
Which many a good tall fellow had destroy'd
So cowardly; and but for these vile guns,
He would himself have been a soldier.
This bald unjointed[13] chat of his, my lord,
I answer'd indirectly, as I said;
And I beseech you, let not his report
Come current for an accusation
Betwixt my love and your high majesty.

BLUNT.   The circumstance consider'd, good my lord,
Whate'er Lord Harry Percy then had said
To such a person and in such a place,
At such a time, with all the rest re-told,
May reasonably die and never rise
To do him wrong, or any way impeach
What then he said,[14] so he unsay it now.

KING.   Why, yet he doth deny his prisoners,
But with[15] proviso and exception,
That we at our own charge shall ransom straight
His brother-in-law, the foolish Mortimer;
Who, on my soul, hath wilfully betray'd

---

11. *grief*] pain.
12. *parmaceti*] a popular form of spermaceti.
13. *unjointed*] incoherent.
14. *impeach What . . . said*] make what he then said matter for accusation.
15. *But with*] save with.

The lives of those that he did lead to fight
Against that great magician, damn'd Glendower,
Whose daughter, as we hear, the Earl of March
Hath lately married. Shall our coffers, then,
Be emptied to redeem a traitor home?
Shall we buy treason? and indent[16] with fears,
When they have lost and forfeited themselves?
No, on the barren mountains let him starve;
For I shall never hold that man my friend
Whose tongue shall ask me for one penny cost
To ransom home revolted Mortimer.

HOT.   Revolted Mortimer!
He never did fall off,[17] my sovereign liege,
But by the chance of war: to prove that true
Needs no more but one tongue for all those wounds,
Those mouthed[18] wounds, which valiantly he took,
When on the gentle Severn's sedgy bank,
In single opposition, hand to hand,
He did confound the best part of an hour
In changing hardiment[19] with great Glendower:
Three times they breathed and three times did they drink,
Upon agreement, of swift Severn's flood;
Who then, affrighted with their bloody looks,
Ran fearfully among the trembling reeds,
And hid his crisp head in the hollow bank
Bloodstained with these valiant combatants.
Never did base and rotten policy
Colour her working with such deadly wounds;
Nor never could the noble Mortimer
Receive so many, and all willingly:
Then let not him be slander'd with revolt.

KING.   Thou dost belie[20] him, Percy, thou dost belie him;
He never did encounter with Glendower:
I tell thee,
He durst as well have met the devil alone
As Owen Glendower for an enemy.
Art thou not ashamed? But, sirrah, henceforth
Let me not hear you speak of Mortimer:

---

16. *indent*] bargain.
17. *fall off*] abandon his allegiance.
18. *mouthed*] gaping.
19. *In changing hardiment*] Exchanging blows.
20. *belie*] praise falsely.

Send me your prisoners with the speediest means,
Or you shall hear in such a kind from me
As will displease you. My Lord Northumberland,
We license your departure with your son.
Send us your prisoners, or you will hear of it.
                        [*Exeunt King Henry, Blunt, and train.*

HOT.   An if the devil come and roar for them,
   I will not send them: I will after straight
   And tell him so; for I will ease my heart,
   Albeit I make a hazard of my head.

NORTH.   What, drunk with choler? stay and pause a while:
   Here comes your uncle.

Re-enter WORCESTER

HOT.   Speak of Mortimer!
   'Zounds, I will speak of him; and let my soul
   Want mercy, if I do not join with him:
   Yea, on his part[21] I'll empty all these veins,
   And shed my dear blood drop by drop in the dust,
   But I will lift the down-trod Mortimer
   As high in the air as this unthankful king,
   As this ingrate and canker'd[22] Bolingbroke.

NORTH.   Brother, the king hath made your nephew mad.

WOR.   Who struck this heat up after I was gone?

HOT.   He will, forsooth, have all my prisoners;
   And when I urged the ransom once again
   Of my wife's brother, then his cheek look'd pale,
   And on my face he turn'd an eye of death,[23]
   Trembling even at the name of Mortimer.

WOR.   I cannot blame him: was not he proclaim'd
   By Richard that dead is the next of blood?[24]

NORTH.   He was; I heard the proclamation:
   And then it was when the unhappy king, —
   Whose wrongs in us[25] God pardon! — did set forth
   Upon his Irish expedition;

---

21. *on his part*] on his behalf.
22. *canker'd*] corroded, malignant.
23. *an eye of death*] a ghastly look of death.
24. *was not he . . . blood?*] Shakespeare here confuses the captured Mortimer with both his brother Roger Mortimer, fourth Earl of March, and his nephew Edmund Mortimer, the fifth Earl. Roger Mortimer was proclaimed heir to the crown by Richard II; when he predeceased the king, the claim was left to his son.
25. *Whose wrongs in us*] Whose wrongs as far as our responsibility for them goes.

From whence he intercepted did return
To be deposed and shortly murdered.
WOR.   And for whose death we in the world's wide mouth
Live scandalized[26] and foully spoken of.
HOT.   But, softly, I pray you; did King Richard then
Proclaim my brother Edmund Mortimer
Heir to the crown?
NORTH.   He did; myself did hear it.
HOT.   Nay, then I cannot blame his cousin king,
That wish'd him on the barren mountains starve.
But shall it be, that you, that set the crown
Upon the head of this forgetful man,
And for his sake wear the detested blot
Of murderous subornation,[27] shall it be,
That you a world of curses undergo,
Being the agents, or base second means,
The cords, the ladder, or the hangman rather?
O, pardon me that I descend so low,
To show the line and the predicament
Wherein you range under this subtle king;
Shall it for shame be spoken in these days,
Or fill up chronicles in time to come,
That men of your nobility and power
Did gage them both in an unjust behalf,
As both of you — God pardon it! — have done,
To put down Richard, that sweet lovely rose,
And plant this thorn, this canker,[28] Bolingbroke?
And shall it in more shame be further spoken,
That you are fool'd, discarded and shook off
By him for whom these shames ye underwent?
No; yet time serves wherein you may redeem
Your banish'd honours, and restore yourselves
Into the good thoughts of the world again,
Revenge the jeering and disdain'd[29] contempt
Of this proud king, who studies day and night
To answer all the debt he owes to you
Even with the bloody payment of your deaths:
Therefore, I say, —
WOR.   Peace, cousin, say no more:

---

26. *scandalized*] defamed.
27. *the detested blot . . . subornation*] the hateful stigma of having instigated murder.
28. *canker*] the dog-rose of the hedge.
29. *disdain'd*] disdainful.

And now I will unclasp a secret book,
And to your quick-conceiving discontents
I'll read you matter deep and dangerous,
As full of peril and adventurous spirit
As to o'er-walk a current roaring loud
On the unsteadfast footing of a spear.
HOT.   If he fall in, good night! or sink or swim:[30]
Send danger from the east unto the west,
So honour cross it from the north to south,
And let them grapple: O, the blood more stirs
To rouse a lion than to start a hare!
NORTH.   Imagination of some great exploit
Drives him beyond the bounds of patience.
HOT.   By heaven, methinks it were an easy leap,
To pluck bright honour from the pale-faced moon,
Or dive into the bottom of the deep,
Where fathom-line could never touch the ground,
And pluck up drowned honour by the locks;
So he that doth redeem her thence might wear
Without corrival[31] all her dignities:
But out upon this half-faced fellowship![32]
WOR.   He apprehends a world of figures here
But not the form of what he should attend.
Good cousin, give me audience for a while.
HOT.   I cry you mercy.
WOR.   Those same noble Scots
That are your prisoners, —
HOT.   I'll keep them all;
By God, he shall not have a Scot of them;
No, if a Scot would save his soul, he shall not:
I'll keep them, by this hand.
WOR.   You start away
And lend no ear unto my purposes.
Those prisoners you shall keep.
HOT.   Nay, I will; that's flat:
He said he would not ransom Mortimer;
Forbad my tongue to speak of Mortimer;
But I will find him when he lies asleep,
And in his ear I'll holla "Mortimer!"

---

30. *or sink or swim*] that is, such a man is doomed if he fall in, whether he sink or swim.
31. *corrival*] rival, competitor.
32. *out upon this half-faced fellowship*] shame on this half-hearted, insincere sort of friendship.

Nay,
I'll have a starling shall be taught to speak
Nothing but "Mortimer," and give it him,
To keep his anger still in motion.

WOR.   Hear you, cousin; a word.

HOT.   All studies here I solemnly defy,[33]
Save how to gall and pinch this Bolingbroke:
And that same sword-and-buckler[34] Prince of Wales,
But that I think his father loves him not
And would be glad he met with some mischance,
I would have him poison'd with a pot of ale.

WOR.   Farewell, kinsman: I'll talk to you
When you are better temper'd to attend.

NORTH.   Why, what a wasp-stung[35] and impatient fool
Art thou to break into this woman's mood,
Tying thine ear to no tongue but thine own!

HOT.   Why, look you, I am whipp'd and scourged with rods,
Nettled, and stung with pismires,[36] when I hear
Of this vile politician, Bolingbroke.
In Richard's time, — what do you call the place? —
A plague upon it, it is in Gloucestershire;
'Twas where the madcap duke his uncle kept,[37]
His uncle York; where I first bow'd my knee
Unto this king of smiles, this Bolingbroke, —
'Sblood! —
When you and he came back from Ravenspurgh.

NORTH.   At Berkley-castle.

HOT.   You say true:
Why, what a candy[38] deal of courtesy
This fawning greyhound then did proffer me!
Look, "when his infant fortune came to age,"
And "gentle Harry Percy," and "kind cousin;"
O, the devil take such cozeners! God forgive me!
Good uncle, tell your tale; I have done.

WOR.   Nay, if you have not, to it again;
We will stay your leisure.

HOT.   I have done, i' faith.

WOR.   Then once more to your Scottish prisoners.

---

33. *defy*] renounce.
34. *sword-and-buckler*] improper arms for a prince, who should carry a rapier and dagger.
35. *wasp-stung*] irritated.
36. *pismires*] ants.
37. *kept*] resided.
38. *candy*] sweet, flattering.

Deliver them up without their ransom straight,
And make the Douglas' son your only mean
For powers[39] in Scotland; which, for divers reasons
Which I shall send you written, be assured,
Will easily be granted. You, my lord,   [*To Northumberland.*
Your son in Scotland being thus employ'd,
Shall secretly into the bosom creep
Of that same noble prelate, well beloved,
The archbishop.
HOT.   Of York, is it not?
WOR.   True; who bears hard
His brother's death at Bristol, the Lord Scroop.
I speak not this in estimation,[40]
As what I think might be, but what I know
Is ruminated, plotted and set down,
And only stays but to behold the face
Of that occasion that shall bring it on.
HOT.   I smell it: upon my life, it will do well.
NORTH.   Before the game is a-foot, thou still let'st slip.[41]
HOT.   Why, it cannot choose but be a noble plot:
And then the power of Scotland and of York,
To join with Mortimer, ha?
WOR.   And so they shall.
HOT.   In faith, it is exceedingly well aim'd.
WOR.   And 'tis no little reason bids us speed,
To save our heads by raising of a head;
For, bear ourselves as even as we can,
The king will always think him in our debt,
And think we think ourselves unsatisfied,
Till he hath found a time to pay us home:
And see already how he doth begin
To make us strangers to his looks of love.
HOT.   He does, he does: we'll be revenged on him.
WOR.   Cousin, farewell: no further go in this
Than I by letters shall direct your course.
When time is ripe, which will be suddenly,
I'll steal to Glendower and Lord Mortimer;
Where you and Douglas and our powers at once,
As I will fashion it, shall happily meet,

---

39. *mean For powers*] means or agent for raising forces.
40. *in estimation*] on conjecture, mere inference.
41. *let'st slip*] i.e., let loose the hounds from their leashes.

     To bear our fortunes in our own strong arms,
      Which now we hold at much uncertainty.
NORTH.   Farewell, good brother: we shall thrive, I trust.
HOT.   Uncle, adieu: O, let the hours be short
      Till fields and blows and groans applaud our sport!   [*Exeunt.*

ACT II.

SCENE I. *Rochester. An Inn Yard.*

Enter a CARRIER *with a lantern in his hand*

FIRST CARRIER. Heigh-ho! An it be not four by the day,[1] I'll be hanged: Charles' wain[2] is over the new chimney, and yet our horse not packed. What, ostler!

OST. [*Within*] Anon, anon.

FIRST CAR. I prithee, Tom, beat Cut's saddle,[3] put a few flocks in the point;[4] poor jade, is wrung in the withers out of all cess.[5]

Enter another CARRIER

SEC. CAR. Peas and beans are as dank here as a dog, and that is the next[6] way to give poor jades the bots:[7] this house is turned upside down since Robin Ostler died.

FIRST CAR. Poor fellow, never joyed since the price of oats rose; it was the death of him.

SEC. CAR. I think this be the most villanous house in all London road for fleas: I am stung like a tench.[8]

FIRST CAR. Like a tench! by the mass, there is ne'er a king christen[9] could be better bit than I have been since the first cock.

SEC. CAR. Why, they will allow us ne'er a jordan, and then we leak in your chimney;[10] and your chamber-lie[11] breeds fleas like a loach.[12]

FIRST CAR. What, ostler! come away and be hanged! come away.

---

1. *by the day*] by the morning light.
2. *Charles' wain*] The constellation called "Ursa Major" or Great Bear.
3. *beat Cut's saddle*] soften the horse's saddle. "Cut" is used as a general name for a horse because of its docked tail.
4. *flocks in the point*] i.e., wool in the pommel of the saddle, so that it won't chafe.
5. *cess*] measure.
6. *next*] surest.
7. *bots*] worms.
8. *stung like a tench*] it was thought that the spots on some fish were due to flea bites.
9. *christen*] in Christendom.
10. *jordan . . . leak . . . chimney*] chamber-pot . . . make water . . . fireplace.
11. *chamber-lie*] urine.
12. *loach*] a highly reproductive fish.

19

SEC. CAR. I have a gammon of bacon and two razes[13] of ginger, to be delivered as far as Charing-cross.

FIRST CAR. God's body! the turkeys in my pannier are quite starved. What, ostler! A plague on thee! hast thou never an eye in thy head? canst not hear? An 'twere not as good deed as drink, to break the pate on thee, I am a very villain. Come, and be hanged! hast no faith in thee?

Enter GADSHILL

GADS. Good morrow, carriers. What's o'clock?

FIRST CAR. I think it be two o'clock.

GADS. I prithee, lend me thy lantern, to see my gelding in the stable.

FIRST CAR. Nay, by God, soft; I know a trick worth two of that, i' faith.

GADS. I pray thee, lend me thine.

SEC. CAR. Ay, when? canst tell?[14] Lend me thy lantern, quoth he? marry, I'll see thee hanged first.

GADS. Sirrah carrier, what time do you mean to come to London?

SEC. CAR. Time enough to go to bed with a candle, I warrant thee. Come, neighbour Mugs, we'll call up the gentlemen: they will along with company, for they have great charge.[15]

[*Exeunt Carriers.*

GADS. What, ho! chamberlain!

CHAM. [*Within*] At hand, quoth pick-purse.[16]

GADS. That's even as fair as — at hand, quoth the chamberlain; for thou variest no more from picking of purses than giving direction doth from labouring; thou layest the plot how.[17]

Enter CHAMBERLAIN

CHAM. Good morrow, Master Gadshill. It holds current that I told you yesternight: there's a franklin[18] in the wild of Kent hath brought three hundred marks with him in gold: I heard him tell it to one of his company last night at supper; a kind of auditor; one that hath abundance of charge too, God knows what. They are up already, and call for eggs and butter: they will away presently.

GADS. Sirrah, if they meet not with Saint Nicholas' clerks,[19] I'll give thee this neck.

CHAM. No, I'll none of it: I pray thee, keep that for the hangman;

13. *razes*] packages.
14. *Ay, when? canst tell?*] Don't you wish I would?
15. *charge*] baggage, goods.
16. *At hand, quoth pick-purse*] a slang phrase for "coming at once."
17. *layest the plot how*] arrange the plot how (robbery is to be effected).
18. *franklin*] yeoman.
19. *Saint Nicholas' clerks*] thieves, highwaymen.

for I know thou worshippest Saint Nicholas as truly as a man of
falsehood may.

GADS. What talkest thou to me of the hangman? if I hang, I'll make a
fat pair of gallows; for if I hang, old Sir John hangs with me, and
thou knowest he is no starveling. Tut! there are other Trojans that
thou dreamest not of, the which for sport sake are content to do the
profession some grace; that would, if matters should be looked into,
for their own credit sake, make all whole. I am joined with no foot
land-rakers,[20] no long-staff sixpenny strikers,[21] none of these mad
mustachio purple-hued malt-worms;[22] but with nobility and tran-
quillity, burgomasters and great oneyers,[23] such as can hold in,[24]
such as will strike sooner than speak, and speak sooner than drink,
and drink sooner than pray: and yet, 'zounds, I lie; for they pray
continually to their saint, the commonwealth; or rather, not pray to
her, but prey on her, for they ride up and down on her and make
her their boots.[25]

CHAM. What, the commonwealth their boots? will she hold out water
in foul way?

GADS. She will, she will; justice hath liquored[26] her. We steal as in
a castle, cock-sure; we have the receipt of fern-seed,[27] we walk
invisible.

CHAM. Nay, by my faith, I think you are more beholding to the night
than to fern-seed for your walking invisible.

GADS. Give me thy hand: thou shalt have a share in our purchase, as I
am a true man.

CHAM. Nay, rather let me have it, as you are a false thief.

GADS. Go to; "homo" is a common name to all men.[28] Bid the ostler
bring my gelding out of the stable. Farewell, you muddy knave.

[Exeunt.

---

20. *foot land-rakers*] common thieves, footpads.
21. *long-staff sixpenny strikers*] thieves who would knock passers-by down with a long stick to
rob them of sixpences.
22. *mustachio purple-hued malt-worms*] drunkards with their mustachios dyed with purple wine.
23. *great oneyers*] possibly an amplification of "great ones."
24. *hold in*] keep their counsel.
25. *make her their boots*] booty, with a pun on "boots."
26. *liquored*] waterproofed, as well as made drunk.
27. *receipt of fern-seed*] Those who carried fern-seed about with them were, it was believed,
thereby rendered invisible.
28. *"homo" . . . all men*] a thief being a man is entitled to that designation.

SCENE II. *The Highway, near Gadshill*

Enter PRINCE HENRY *and* POINS

POINS. Come, shelter, shelter: I have removed Falstaff's horse, and he frets like a gummed velvet.[1]

PRINCE. Stand close.

Enter FALSTAFF

FAL. Poins! Poins, and be hanged! Poins!

PRINCE. Peace, ye fat-kidneyed rascal! what a brawling dost thou keep!

FAL. Where's Poins, Hal?

PRINCE. He is walked up to the top of the hill: I'll go seek him.

FAL. I am accursed to rob in that thief's company: the rascal hath removed my horse, and tied him I know not where. If I travel but four foot by the squier[2] further afoot, I shall break my wind. Well, I doubt not but to die a fair death for all this, if I 'scape hanging for killing that rogue. I have forsworn his company hourly any time this two and twenty years, and yet I am bewitched with the rogue's company. If the rascal have not given me medicines[3] to make me love him, I'll be hanged; it could not be else; I have drunk medicines. Poins! Hal! a plague upon you both! Bardolph! Peto! I'll starve ere I'll rob a foot further. An 'twere not as good a deed as drink, to turn true man and to leave these rogues, I am the veriest varlet that ever chewed with a tooth. Eight yards of uneven ground is threescore and ten miles afoot with me; and the stony-hearted villains know it well enough: a plague upon it when thieves cannot be true one to another! [*They whistle.*] Whew! A plague upon you all! Give me my horse, you rogues; give me my horse, and be hanged!

PRINCE. Peace, ye fat-guts! lie down; lay thine ear close to the ground and list if thou canst hear the tread of travellers.

FAL. Have you any levers to lift me up again, being down? 'Sblood, I'll not bear mine own flesh so far afoot again for all the coin in thy father's exchequer. What a plague mean ye to colt[4] me thus?

PRINCE. Thou liest; thou art not colted, thou art uncolted.

FAL. I prithee, good Prince Hal, help me to my horse, good king's son.

---

1. *frets . . . velvet*] inferior velvets would easily fret or fray.
2. *squier*] square, measure.
3. *medicines*] love philtres or powders.
4. *colt*] trick.

PRINCE. Out, ye rogue! shall I be your ostler?

FAL. Go hang thyself in thine own heir-apparent garters! If I be ta'en, I'll peach[5] for this. An I have not ballads made on you all and sung to filthy tunes, let a cup of sack be my poison: when a jest is so forward, and afoot too! I hate it.

Enter GADSHILL, BARDOLPH and PETO with him

GADS. Stand.

FAL. So I do, against my will.

POINS. O, 'tis our setter:[6] I know his voice. Bardolph, what news?

BARD. Case ye,[7] case ye; on with your vizards: there's money of the king's coming down the hill; 'tis going to the king's exchequer.

FAL. You lie, ye rogue; 'tis going to the king's tavern.

GADS. There's enough to make us all.

FAL. To be hanged.

PRINCE. Sirs, you four shall front them in the narrow lane; Ned Poins and I will walk lower: if they 'scape from your encounter, then they light on us.

PETO. How many be there of them?

GADS. Some eight or ten.

FAL. 'Zounds, will they not rob us?

PRINCE. What, a coward, Sir John Paunch?

FAL. Indeed, I am not John of Gaunt,[8] your grandfather; but yet no coward, Hal.

PRINCE. Well, we leave that to the proof.

POINS. Sirrah Jack, thy horse stands behind the hedge: when thou needest him, there thou shalt find him. Farewell, and stand fast.

FAL. Now cannot I strike him, if I should be hanged.

PRINCE. Ned, where are our disguises?

POINS. Here, hard by: stand close.   [Exeunt Prince and Poins.

FAL. Now, my masters, happy man be his dole,[9] say I: every man to his business.

Enter the Travellers

FIRST TRAV. Come, neighbour: the boy shall lead our horses down the hill; we'll walk afoot awhile, and ease our legs.

THIEVES. Stand!

TRAVELLERS. Jesus bless us!

---

5. *peach*] give information.
6. *setter*] organizer of a robbery.
7. *Case ye*] Cover yourselves.
8. *Gaunt*] a pun on *gaunt*, thin.
9. *happy man be his dole*] good fortune be his lot.

FAL.   Strike; down with them; cut the villains' throats: ah! whoreson caterpillars![10] bacon-fed knaves! they hate us youth: down with them;
fleece them.

TRAVELLERS.   O, we are undone, both we and ours for ever!

FAL.   Hang ye, gorbellied[11] knaves, are ye undone? No, ye fat chuffs;[12]
I would your store were here! On, bacons,[13] on! What, ye knaves!
young men must live. You are grandjurors, are ye? we'll jure[14] ye,
'faith.   [*Here they rob them and bind them. Exeunt.*

Re-enter PRINCE HENRY *and* POINS *disguised*

PRINCE.   The thieves have bound the true men. Now could thou and I
rob the thieves and go merrily to London, it would be argument[15]
for a week, laughter for a month and a good jest for ever.

POINS.   Stand close; I hear them coming.

Enter the Thieves *again*

FAL.   Come, my masters, let us share, and then to horse before day. An
the Prince and Poins be not two arrant cowards, there's no equity
stirring: there's no more valour in that Poins than in a wild-duck.

PRINCE.   Your money!

POINS.   Villains!

       [*As they are sharing, the Prince and Poins set upon them;
they all run away; and Falstaff, after a blow or two,
runs away too, leaving the booty behind them.*]

PRINCE.   Got with much ease. Now merrily to horse:
The thieves are all scatter'd and possess'd with fear
So strongly that they dare not meet each other;
Each takes his fellow for an officer.
Away, good Ned. Falstaff sweats to death,
And lards the lean earth as he walks along:
Were 't not for laughing, I should pity him.

POINS.   How the rogue roar'd!   [*Exeunt.*

---

10. *caterpillars*] idlers, parasites.
11. *gorbellied*] potbellied, paunchy.
12. *chuffs*] rich but miserly boors.
13. *bacons*] swine.
14. *jure*] Falstaff coins the verb out of "grandjurors."
15. *argument*] theme of talk.

SCENE III. *Warkworth Castle.*

Enter HOTSPUR *solus, reading a letter*

HOT. "But, for mine own part, my lord, I could be well contented to
be there, in respect of the love I bear your house." He could be
contented: why is he not, then? In respect of the love he bears our
house: he shows in this, he loves his own barn better than he loves
our house. Let me see some more. "The purpose you undertake
is dangerous;" — why, that's certain: 'tis dangerous to take a cold,
to sleep, to drink; but I tell you, my lord fool, out of this nettle,
danger, we pluck this flower, safety. "The purpose you undertake
is dangerous; the friends you have named uncertain; the time itself
unsorted;[1] and your whole plot too light for the counterpoise of so
great an opposition." Say you so, say you so? I say unto you again,
you are a shallow cowardly hind, and you lie. What a lack-brain is
this! By the Lord, our plot is a good plot as ever was laid; our friends
true and constant: a good plot, good friends, and full of expectation;
an excellent plot, very good friends. What a frosty-spirited rogue
is this! Why, my lord of York commends the plot and the general
course of the action. 'Zounds, an I were now by this rascal, I could
brain him with his lady's fan. Is there not my father, my uncle,
and myself? lord Edmund Mortimer, my lord of York, and Owen
Glendower? is there not besides the Douglas? have I not all their
letters to meet me in arms by the ninth of the next month? and are
they not some of them set forward already? What a pagan rascal is
this! an infidel! Ha! you shall see now in very sincerity of fear and
cold heart, will he to the king, and lay open all our proceedings.
O, I could divide myself, and go to buffets,[2] for moving such a dish
of skim milk with so honourable an action! Hang him! let him tell
the king: we are prepared. I will set forward to-night.

Enter LADY PERCY

How now, Kate! I must leave you within these two hours.
LADY.   O, my good Lord, why are you thus alone?
For what offence have I this fortnight been
A banish'd woman from my Harry's bed?
Tell me, sweet Lord, what is 't that takes from thee

---

1. *unsorted*] ill-chosen, unsuitable.
2. *I could . . . go to buffets*] I could fight against myself.

Thy stomach, pleasure, and thy golden sleep?
Why dost thou bend thine eyes upon the earth,
And start so often when thou sit'st alone?
Why hast thou lost the fresh blood in thy cheeks,
And given my treasures and my rights of thee[3]
To thick-eyed musing and cursed melancholy?
In thy faint slumbers I by thee have watch'd,
And heard thee murmur tales of iron wars;
Speak terms of manage to thy bounding steed;
Cry "Courage! to the field!" And thou hast talk'd
Of sallies and retires,[4] of trenches, tents,
Of palisadoes, frontiers, parapets,
Of basilisks, of cannon, culverin,[5]
Of prisoners' ransom, and of soldiers slain,
And all the currents of a heady fight.
Thy spirit within thee hath been so at war
And thus hath so bestirr'd thee in thy sleep,
That beads of sweat have stood upon thy brow,
Like bubbles in a late-disturbed stream;
And in thy face strange motions have appear'd,
Such as we see when men restrain their breath
On some great sudden hest.[6] O, what portents are these?
Some heavy business hath my lord in hand,
And I must know it, else he loves me not.

HOT.   What, ho!

Enter SERVANT

Is Gilliams with the packet gone?
SERV.   He is, my lord, an hour ago.
HOT.   Hath Butler brought those horses from the sheriff?
SERV.   One horse, my lord, he brought even now.
HOT.   What horse? a roan, a crop-ear, is it not?
SERV.   It is, my lord.
HOT.   That roan shall be my throne.
    Well, I will back him[7] straight: O esperance![8]
    Bid Butler lead him forth into the park.   [*Exit Servant.*
LADY.   But hear you, my lord.

---

3. *my treasures . . . thee*] my treasured wifely rights.
4. *sallies and retires*] sorties and retreats.
5. *basilisks . . . culverin*] large pieces of ordnance . . . small cannon.
6. *hest*] command.
7. *back him*] mount him.
8. *O esperance*] O hope; the motto of the Percy family.

HOT.   What say'st thou, my lady?
LADY.   What is it carries you away?[9]
HOT.   Why, my horse, my love, my horse.
LADY.   Out, you mad-headed ape!
    A weasel hath not such a deal of spleen
    As you are toss'd with. In faith,
    I'll know your business, Harry, that I will.
    I fear my brother Mortimer doth stir
    About his title, and hath sent for you
    To line[10] his enterprise: but if you go —
HOT.   So far afoot, I shall be weary, love.
LADY.   Come, come, you paraquito,[11] answer me
    Directly unto this question that I ask:
    In faith, I'll break thy little finger, Harry,
    An if thou wilt not tell me all things true.
HOT.   Away,
    Away, you trifler! Love! I love thee not,
    I care not for thee, Kate: this is no world
    To play with mammets[12] and to tilt with lips:
    We must have bloody noses and crack'd crowns,
    And pass them current too.[13] God's me, my horse!
    What say'st thou, Kate! what wouldst thou have with me?
LADY.   Do you not love me? do you not, indeed?
    Well, do not then; for since you love me not,
    I will not love myself. Do you not love me?
    Nay, tell me if you speak in jest or no.
HOT.   Come, wilt thou see me ride?
    And when I am o' horseback, I will swear
    I love thee infinitely. But hark you, Kate;
    I must not have you henceforth question me
    Whither I go, nor reason whereabout:
    Whither I must, I must; and, to conclude,
    This evening must I leave you, gentle Kate.
    I know you wise, but yet no farther wise
    Than Harry Percy's wife: constant you are,
    But yet a woman: and for secrecy,
    No lady closer; for I well believe
    Thou wilt not utter what thou dost not know;

---

9. *carries you away*] distracts, transports you.
10. *line*] strengthen, support.
11. *paraquito*] little parrot.
12. *mammets*] puppets, dolls.
13. *crowns . . . current*] a quibble on the double meaning of the word "crowns" as "heads" and "coins."

And so far will I trust thee, gentle Kate.

LADY.   How! so far?

HOT.   Not an inch further. But hark you, Kate:
Whither I go, thither shall you go too;
To-day will I set forth, to-morrow you.
Will this content you, Kate?

LADY.   It must of force.   [*Exeunt.*

SCENE IV.   *The Boar's-Head Tavern in Eastcheap.*

Enter the PRINCE, *and* POINS

PRINCE.   Ned, prithee, come out of that fat[1] room, and lend me thy hand
to laugh a little.

POINS.   Where hast been, Hal?

PRINCE.   With three or four loggerheads amongst three or fourscore
hogsheads. I have sounded the very base-string of humility. Sirrah,
I am sworn brother to a leash of drawers;[2] and can call them all
by their christen names, as Tom, Dick, and Francis. They take it
already upon their salvation, that though I be but Prince of Wales,
yet I am the king of courtesy; and tell me flatly I am no proud
Jack, like Falstaff, but a Corinthian,[3] a lad of mettle, a good boy,
by the Lord, so they call me, and when I am king of England, I
shall command all the good lads in Eastcheap. They call drinking deep, dyeing scarlet; and when you breathe in your water-
ing, they cry "hem!" and bid you play it off. To conclude, I am
so good a proficient in one quarter of an hour, that I can drink
with any tinker in his own language during my life. I tell thee,
Ned, thou hast lost much honour, that thou wert not with me
in this action. But, sweet Ned, — to sweeten which name of Ned,
I give thee this pennyworth of sugar, clapped even now into my
hand by an under-skinker,[4] one that never spake other English
in his life than "Eight shillings and sixpence," and "You are wel-

---

1. *fat*] stuffy; also, vat room.
2. *leash of drawers*] three tapsters.
3. *a Corinthian*] a buck, a blood, a young man of spirit.
4. *under-skinker*] inferior tapster or pot-boy.

come," with this shrill addition, "Anon, anon, sir! Score a pint of bastard[5] in the Half-moon,"[6] or so. But, Ned, to drive away the time till Falstaff come, I prithee, do thou stand in some by-room, while I question my puny drawer to what end he gave me the sugar; and do thou never leave calling "Francis," that his tale to me may be nothing but "Anon." Step aside, and I'll show thee a precedent.

POINS. Francis!

PRINCE. Thou art perfect.

POINS. Francis!   [*Exit Poins.*

Enter FRANCIS

FRAN. Anon, anon, sir. Look down into the Pomgarnet,[7] Ralph.

PRINCE. Come hither, Francis.

FRAN. My lord?

PRINCE. How long hast thou to serve, Francis?

FRAN. Forsooth, five years, and as much as to —

POINS. [*Within*] Francis!

FRAN. Anon, anon, sir.

PRINCE. Five year! by 'r lady, a long lease for the clinking of pewter. But, Francis, darest thou be so valiant as to play the coward with thy indenture and show it a fair pair of heels and run from it?

FRAN. O Lord, sir, I'll be sworn upon all the books in England, I could find in my heart.

POINS. [*Within*] Francis!

FRAN. Anon, sir.

PRINCE. How old art thou, Francis?

FRAN. Let me see — about Michaelmas next I shall be —

POINS. [*Within*] Francis!

FRAN. Anon, sir. Pray stay a little, my lord.

PRINCE. Nay, but hark you, Francis: for the sugar thou gavest me, 'twas a pennyworth, was 't not?

FRAN. O Lord, I would it had been two!

PRINCE. I will give thee for it a thousand pound: ask me when thou wilt, and thou shalt have it.

POINS. [*Within*] Francis!

FRAN. Anon, anon.

PRINCE. Anon, Francis? No, Francis; but to-morrow, Francis; or Francis, o' Thursday; or indeed, Francis, when thou wilt. But, Francis!

FRAN. My lord?

---

5. *bastard*] a sweet Spanish wine.
6. *Half-moon*] the name of a room in the inn.
7. *Pomgarnet*] another room in the inn.

PRINCE. Wilt thou rob this leathern jerkin, crystal-button, not-pated,[8] agate-ring, puke-stocking, caddis-garter, smooth-tongue, Spanish-pouch,[9] —

FRAN. O lord, sir, who do you mean?

PRINCE. Why, then, your brown bastard is your only drink; for look you, Francis, your white canvas doublet will sully: in Barbary, sir, it cannot come to so much.[10]

FRAN. What, sir?

POINS. [*Within*] Francis!

PRINCE. Away, you rogue! dost thou not hear them call?

> [*Here they both call him; the drawer stands amazed, not knowing which way to go.*]

Enter VINTNER

VINT. What, standest thou still, and hearest such a calling? Look to the guests within. [*Exit Francis.*] My lord, old Sir John, with half-a-dozen more, are at the door: shall I let them in?

PRINCE. Let them alone awhile, and then open the door. [*Exit Vintner.*] Poins!

Re-enter POINS

POINS. Anon, anon, sir.

PRINCE. Sirrah, Falstaff and the rest of the thieves are at the door: shall we be merry?

POINS. As merry as crickets, my lad. But hark ye; what cunning match have you made with this jest of the drawer? come, what's the issue?

PRINCE. I am now of all humours that have showed themselves humours since the old days of goodman Adam to the pupil age of this present twelve o'clock at midnight.

Re-enter FRANCIS

What's o'clock, Francis?

FRAN. Anon, anon, sir.   [*Exit.*

PRINCE. That ever this fellow should have fewer words than a parrot, and yet the son of a woman! His industry is up-stairs and down-stairs; his eloquence the parcel[11] of a reckoning. I am not yet of Percy's mind, the Hotspur of the north; he that kills me some six or seven dozen of Scots at a breakfast, washes his hands, and says to his wife "Fie upon this quiet life! I want work." "O my sweet Harry,"

---

8. *not-pated*] crop-haired. The prince is describing the vintner, the boy's master.
9. *Spanish-pouch*] with a paunch filled with Spanish wine.
10. *Why ... much*] The Prince is here mystifying Francis by the irrelevance and incoherence of his remarks.
11. *parcel*] items.

says she, "how many hast thou killed to-day?" "Give my roan horse a drench," says he; and answers "Some fourteen," an hour after; "a trifle, a trifle." I prithee, call in Falstaff: I'll play Percy, and that damned brawn shall play Dame Mortimer his wife. "Rivo!"[12] says the drunkard. Call in ribs, call in tallow.

Enter FALSTAFF, GADSHILL, BARDOLPH, *and* PETO; FRANCIS *following with wine*

POINS. Welcome, Jack: where hast thou been?

FAL. A plague of all cowards, I say, and a vengeance too! marry, and amen! Give me a cup of sack, boy. Ere I lead this life long, I'll sew nether stocks[13] and mend them and foot them too. A plague of all cowards! Give me a cup of sack, rogue. Is there no virtue extant?
[*He drinks.*

PRINCE. Didst thou never see Titan[14] kiss a dish of butter? pitiful-hearted Titan,[15] that melted at the sweet tale of the sun's! if thou didst, then behold that compound.

FAL. You rogue, here's lime in this sack[16] too: there is nothing but roguery to be found in villanous man: yet a coward is worse than a cup of sack with lime in it. A villanous coward! Go thy ways, old Jack; die when thou wilt, if manhood, good manhood, be not forgot upon the face of the earth, then am I a shotten herring.[17] There lives not three good men unhanged in England; and one of them is fat, and grows old: God help the while! a bad world, I say. I would I were a weaver;[18] I could sing psalms or any thing. A plague of all cowards, I say still.

PRINCE. How now, wool-sack! what mutter you?

FAL. A king's son! If I do not beat thee out of thy kingdom with a dagger of lath,[19] and drive all thy subjects afore thee like a flock of wild-geese, I'll never wear hair on my face more. You Prince of Wales!

PRINCE. Why, you whoreson round man, what's the matter?

FAL. Are not you a coward? answer me to that: and Poins there?

POINS. 'Zounds, ye fat paunch, an ye call me coward, by the Lord, I'll stab thee.

FAL. I call thee coward! I'll see thee damned ere I call thee coward: but

---

12. *Rivo!*] An exclamation, probably of Spanish origin, common among Elizabethan topers.
13. *nether stocks*] stockings.
14. *Titan*] the sun.
15. *pitiful-hearted Titan*] it has been suggested that substituting "butter" for this second "Titan" will make sense of this barely intelligible passage.
16. *lime in this sack*] i.e., added to make the drink sparkle.
17. *a shotten herring*] a herring that has shed its roe.
18. *weaver*] many weavers were psalm-singing Calvinists from the Netherlands.
19. *dagger of lath*] the weapon of Vice in the old morality plays.

I would give a thousand pound I could run as fast as thou canst. You are straight enough in the shoulders, you care not who sees your back: call you that backing of your friends? A plague upon such backing! give me them that will face me. Give me a cup of sack: I am a rogue, if I drunk to-day.

PRINCE. O villain! thy lips are scarce wiped since thou drunkest last.
FAL. All's one for that. [*He drinks.*] A plague of all cowards, still say I.
PRINCE. What's the matter?
FAL. What's the matter! there be four of us here have ta'en a thousand pounds this day morning.
PRINCE. Where is it, Jack? where is it?
FAL. Where is it! taken from us it is: a hundred upon poor four of us.
PRINCE. What, a hundred, man?
FAL. I am a rogue, if I were not at half-sword[20] with a dozen of them two hours together. I have 'scaped by miracle. I am eight times thrust through the doublet, four through the hose; my buckler cut through and through; my sword hacked like a hand-saw — ecce signum! I never dealt better since I was a man: all would not do. A plague of all cowards! Let them speak: if they speak more or less than truth, they are villains and the sons of darkness.
PRINCE. Speak, sirs; how was it?
GADS. We four set upon some dozen —
FAL. Sixteen at least, my lord.
GADS. And bound them.
PETO. No, no, they were not bound.
FAL. You rogue, they were bound, every man of them; or I am a Jew else, an Ebrew Jew.
GADS. As we were sharing, some six or seven fresh men set upon us —
FAL. And unbound the rest, and then come in the other.
PRINCE. What, fought you with them all?
FAL. All! I know not what you call all; but if I fought not with fifty of them, I am a bunch of radish: if there were not two or three and fifty upon poor old Jack, then am I no two-legged creature.
PRINCE. Pray God you have not murdered some of them.
FAL. Nay, that's past praying for: I have peppered two of them; two I am sure I have paid, two rogues in buckram suits. I tell thee what, Hal, if I tell thee a lie, spit in my face, call me horse. Thou knowest my old ward;[21] here I lay, and thus I bore my point. Four rogues in buckram let drive at me —
PRINCE. What, four? thou saidst but two even now.
FAL. Four, Hal; I told thee four.

---

20. *at half-sword*] at close quarters.
21. *my old ward*] my old guard, my favourite posture of defense.

POINS. Ay, ay, he said four.

FAL. These four came all a-front, and mainly[22] thrust at me. I made me no more ado but took all their seven points in my target, thus.

PRINCE. Seven? why, there were but four even now.

FAL. In buckram?

POINS. Ay, four, in buckram suits.

FAL. Seven, by these hilts, or I am a villain else.

PRINCE. Prithee, let him alone; we shall have more anon.

FAL. Dost thou hear me, Hal?

PRINCE. Ay, and mark thee too, Jack.

FAL. Do so, for it is worth the listening to. These nine in buckram that I told thee of, —

PRINCE. So, two more already.

FAL. Their points being broken, —

POINS. Down fell their hose.[23]

FAL. Began to give me ground: but I followed me close, came in foot and hand; and with a thought seven of the eleven I paid.

PRINCE. O monstrous! eleven buckram men grown out of two!

FAL. But, as the devil would have it, three misbegotten knaves in Kendal green came at my back and let drive at me; for it was so dark, Hal, that thou couldst not see thy hand.

PRINCE. These lies are like their father that begets them; gross as a mountain, open, palpable. Why, thou clay-brained guts, thou knotty-pated[24] fool, thou whoreson, obscene, greasy tallow-catch,[25] —

FAL. What, art thou mad? art thou mad? is not the truth the truth?

PRINCE. Why, how couldst thou know these men in Kendal green,[26] when it was so dark thou couldst not see thy hand? come, tell us your reason: what sayest thou to this?

POINS. Come, your reason, Jack, your reason.

FAL. What, upon compulsion? 'Zounds, an I were at the strappado,[27] or all the racks in the world, I would not tell you on compulsion. Give you a reason on compulsion! if reasons were as plentiful as blackberries, I would give no man a reason upon compulsion, I.

PRINCE. I'll be no longer guilty of this sin; this sanguine coward, this bed-presser, this horse-back-breaker, this huge hill of flesh, —

FAL. 'Sblood, you starveling, you elf-skin, you dried neat's tongue, you

---

22. *mainly*] violently.
23. *Their points . . . hose*] "Points" has the double meaning of "sword-points" and the "tags" or laces, which attached the (trunk) hose to the doublet.
24. *knotty-pated*] blockheaded.
25. *tallow-catch*] apparently a receptacle for tallow-grease.
26. *Kendal green*] green woollen cloth worn by foresters.
27. *strappado*] a kind of torture.

bull's pizzle, you stock-fish! O for breath to utter what is like thee! you tailor's yard, you sheath, you bow-case, you vile standing tuck,[28] —

PRINCE. Well, breathe a while, and then to it again: and when thou hast tired thyself in base comparisons, hear me speak but this.

POINS. Mark, Jack.

PRINCE. We two saw you four set on four and bound them, and were masters of their wealth. Mark now, how a plain tale shall put you down. Then did we two set on you four; and, with a word, out-faced you from your prize, and have it; yea, and can show it you here in the house: and, Falstaff, you carried your guts away as nimbly, with as quick dexterity, and roared for mercy, and still run and roared, as ever I heard bull-calf. What a slave art thou, to hack thy sword as thou hast done, and then say it was in fight! What trick, what device, what starting-hole,[29] canst thou now find out to hide thee from this open and apparent shame?

POINS. Come, let's hear, Jack; what trick hast thou now?

FAL. By the Lord, I knew ye as well as he that made ye. Why, hear you, my masters: was it for me to kill the heir-apparent? should I turn upon the true prince? why, thou knowest I am as valiant as Hercules: but beware instinct; the lion will not touch the true prince. Instinct is a great matter; I was now a coward on instinct. I shall think the better of myself and thee during my life; I for a valiant lion, and thou for a true prince. But, by the Lord, lads, I am glad you have the money. Hostess, clap to the doors: watch to-night, pray to-morrow. Gallants, lads, boys, hearts of gold, all the titles of good fellowship come to you! What, shall we be merry? shall we have a play extempore?

PRINCE. Content; and the argument shall be thy running away.

FAL. Ah, no more of that, Hal, an thou lovest me!

Enter Hostess

HOST. O Jesu, my lord the prince!

PRINCE. How now, my lady the hostess! what sayest thou to me?

HOST. Marry, my lord, there is a nobleman of the court at door would speak with you: he says he comes from your father.

PRINCE. Give him as much as will make him a royal man,[30] and send him back again to my mother.

---

28. *standing tuck*] a rapier standing on end.
29. *starting-hole*] shelter in which a hunted animal takes refuge.
30. *royal*] a pun on the words "noble" and "royal," which were the names of coins. A "noble" was worth 6s. 8d., while the "royal" was of the value of 10s. The prince jestingly suggests that the difference between those two sums defines the interval between a "nobleman" and a "royal man."

FAL. What manner of man is he?

HOST. An old man.

FAL. What doth gravity out of his bed at midnight? Shall I give him his
answer?

PRINCE. Prithee, do, Jack.

FAL. Faith, and I'll send him packing.   [*Exit.*

PRINCE. Now, sirs: by 'r lady, you fought fair; so did you, Peto; so did
you, Bardolph: you are lions too, you ran away upon instinct, you
will not touch the true prince; no, fie!

BARD. Faith, I ran when I saw others run.

PRINCE. Faith, tell me now in earnest, how came Falstaff's sword so
hacked?

PETO. Why, he hacked it with his dagger, and said he would swear truth
out of England but he would make you believe it was done in fight,
and persuaded us to do the like.

BARD. Yea, and to tickle our noses with spear-grass to make them bleed,
and then to beslubber our garments with it and swear it was the
blood of true men. I did that I did not this seven year before, I
blushed to hear his monstrous devices.

PRINCE. O villain, thou stolest a cup of sack eighteen years ago, and
wert taken with the manner,[31] and ever since thou hast blushed
extempore. Thou hadst fire[32] and sword on thy side, and yet thou
rannest away: what instinct hadst thou for it?

BARD. My lord, do you see these meteors? do you behold these exhalations?[33]

PRINCE. I do.

BARD. What think you they portend?

PRINCE. Hot livers and cold purses.[34]

BARD. Choler, my lord, if rightly taken.

PRINCE. No, if rightly taken, halter.

Re-enter FALSTAFF

Here comes lean Jack, here comes bare-bone. How now, my sweet
creature of bombast![35] How long is 't ago, Jack, since thou sawest
thine own knee?

FAL. My own knee! when I was about thy years, Hal, I was not an eagle's
talon in the waist; I could have crept into any alderman's thumb-
ring: a plague of sighing and grief! it blows a man up like a bladder.

---

31. *with the manner*] "in flagrante delicto," in the very act.
32. *Thou hadst fire*] a reference to Bardolph's inflamed countenance.
33. *exhalations*] meteors; here, the red blotches on his face.
34. *Hot livers and cold purses*] Hard drinking and empty purses.
35. *bombast*] stuffing or padding of clothes.

There's villanous news abroad: here was Sir John Bracy from your
father; you must to the court in the morning. That same mad fellow
of the north, Percy, and he of Wales, that gave Amamon the bastinado,[36] and made Lucifer cuckold, and swore the devil his true
liegeman upon the cross of a Welsh hook[37] — what a plague call
you him?

POINS. O, Glendower.

FAL. Owen, Owen, the same; and his son-in-law Mortimer, and old
Northumberland, and that sprightly Scot of Scots, Douglas, that
runs o' horseback up a hill perpendicular, —

PRINCE. He that rides at high speed and with his pistol kills a sparrow
flying.

FAL. You have hit it.

PRINCE. So did he never the sparrow.

FAL. Well, that rascal hath good mettle in him; he will not run.

PRINCE. Why, what a rascal art thou then, to praise him so for running!

FAL. O' horseback, ye cuckoo; but afoot he will not budge a foot.

PRINCE. Yes, Jack, upon instinct.

FAL. I grant ye, upon instinct. Well, he is there too, and one Mordake,
and a thousand blue-caps[38] more: Worcester is stolen away to-night;
thy father's beard is turned white with the news: you may buy land
now as cheap as stinking mackerel.

PRINCE. Why, then, it is like, if there come a hot June and this civil
buffeting hold, we shall buy maidenheads as they buy hob-nails, by
the hundreds.

FAL. By the mass, lad, thou sayest true; it is like we shall have good
trading that way. But tell me, Hal, art not thou horrible afeard?
thou being heir-apparent, could the world pick thee out three such
enemies again as that fiend Douglas, that spirit Percy, and that
devil Glendower? art thou not horribly afraid? doth not thy blood
thrill at it?

PRINCE. Not a whit, i' faith; I lack some of thy instinct.

FAL. Well, thou wilt be horribly chid to-morrow when thou comest to
thy father: if thou love me, practise an answer.

PRINCE. Do thou stand for my father, and examine me upon the
particulars of my life.

FAL. Shall I? content: this chair shall be my state,[39] this dagger my
sceptre, and this cushion my crown.

36. *Amamon . . . bastinado*] the name of an evil spirit . . . a stiff cudgeling.
37. *Welsh hook*] a long-handled weapon with a curved blade.
38. *blue-caps*] the blue bonnets distinctive of Scottish troops.
39. *my state*] my canopied throne.

PRINCE. Thy state is taken for a joined-stool, thy golden sceptre for a leaden dagger, and thy precious rich crown for a pitiful bald crown!

FAL. Well, an the fire of grace be not quite out of thee, now shalt thou be moved. Give me a cup of sack to make my eyes look red, that it may be thought I have wept; for I must speak in passion, and I will do it in King Cambyses' vein.[40]

PRINCE. Well, here is my leg.[41]

FAL. And here is my speech. Stand aside, nobility.

HOST. O Jesu, this is excellent sport, i' faith!

FAL. Weep not, sweet queen; for trickling tears are vain.

HOST. O, the father, how he holds his countenance!

FAL. For God's sake, lords, convey my tristful queen;[42] For tears do stop the flood-gates of her eyes.

HOST. O Jesu, he doth it as like one of these harlotry[43] players as ever I see!

FAL. Peace, good pint-pot; peace, good tickle-brain.[44] Harry, I do not only marvel where thou spendest thy time, but also how thou art accompanied: for though the camomile, the more it is trodden on the faster it grows, yet youth, the more it is wasted the sooner it wears.[45] That thou art my son, I have partly thy mother's word, partly my own opinion, but chiefly a villanous trick of thine eye, and a foolish hanging of thy nether lip, that doth warrant me. If then thou be son to me, here lies the point; why, being son to me, art thou so pointed at? Shall the blessed sun of heaven prove a micher[46] and eat blackberries? a question not to be asked. Shall the son of England prove a thief and take purses? a question to be asked. There is a thing, Harry, which thou hast often heard of, and it is known to many in our land by the name of pitch: this pitch, as ancient writers[47] do report, doth defile; so doth the company thou keepest: for, Harry, now I do not speak to thee in drink but in tears, not in pleasure but in passion, not in words only, but in woes also: and yet there is a virtuous man whom I have often noted in thy company, but I know not his name.

PRINCE. What manner of man, an it like your majesty?

FAL. A goodly portly man, i' faith, and a corpulent; of a cheerful look, a pleasing eye, and a most noble carriage; and, as I think, his age

---

40. *in King Cambyses' vein*] in the ranting style of Thomas Preston's tragedy *Cambises*.
41. *leg*] bow.
42. *convey my tristful queen*] lead away my sorrowful queen.
43. *harlotry*] vagabond.
44. *tickle-brain*] a nickname of strong liquor.
45. *the camomile . . . sooner it wears*] These sentences parody a passage in Lyly's *Euphues*.
46. *a micher*] a truant.
47. *ancient writers*] Cf. *Ecclesiasticus* 13:1: "He that toucheth pitch shall be defiled therewith."

some fifty, or, by 'r lady, inclining to three score; and now I remember me, his name is Falstaff: if that man should be lewdly
given,[48] he deceiveth me; for, Harry, I see virtue in his looks. If then
the tree may be known by the fruit, as the fruit by the tree, then,
peremptorily I speak it, there is virtue in that Falstaff; him keep
with, the rest banish. And tell me now, thou naughty varlet, tell me,
where hast thou been this month?

PRINCE. Dost thou speak like a king? Do thou stand for me, and I'll play
my father.

FAL. Depose me? if thou dost it half so gravely, so majestically, both in
word and matter, hang me up by the heels for a rabbit-sucker or a
poulter's hare.[49]

PRINCE. Well, here I am set.

FAL. And here I stand: judge, my masters.

PRINCE. Now, Harry, whence come you?

FAL. My noble lord; from Eastcheap.

PRINCE. The complaints I hear of thee are grievous.

FAL. 'Sblood, my lord, they are false: nay, I'll tickle ye for a young
prince, i' faith.

PRINCE. Swearest thou, ungracious boy? henceforth ne'er look on me.
Thou art violently carried away from grace: there is a devil haunts
thee in the likeness of an old fat man; a tun of man is thy companion. Why dost thou converse with that trunk of humours, that
bolting-hutch[50] of beastliness, that swollen parcel of dropsies, that
huge bombard[51] of sack, that stuffed cloak-bag of guts, that roasted
Manningtree ox[52] with the pudding in his belly, that reverend vice,
that grey iniquity,[53] that father ruffian, that vanity in years? Wherein
is he good, but to taste sack and drink it? wherein neat and cleanly,
but to carve a capon and eat it? wherein cunning, but in craft?
wherein crafty, but in villany? wherein villanous, but in all things?
wherein worthy, but in nothing?

FAL. I would your grace would take me with you: whom means your
grace?

PRINCE. That villanous abominable misleader of youth, Falstaff, that
old white-bearded Satan.

FAL. My lord, the man I know.

PRINCE. I know thou dost.

---

48. *lewdly given*] inclined to wickedness.
49. *a rabbit-sucker or a poulter's hare*] a sucking rabbit or a poulterer's hare.
50. *bolting-hutch*] flour bin.
51. *bombard*] leather jug or black-jack.
52. *Manningtree ox*] The agricultural town of Manningtree in Essex seems to have been
    famous for its breed of fat oxen. A famous fair was held there annually.
53. *vice . . . iniquity*] alternative names of a clownish character in the old morality plays.

FAL.   But to say I know more harm in him than in myself, were to say
       more than I know. That he is old, the more the pity, his white hairs
       do witness it; but that he is, saving your reverence, a whoremaster,
       that I utterly deny. If sack and sugar be a fault, God help the wicked!
       if to be old and merry be a sin, then many an old host that I know
       is damned: if to be fat be to be hated, then Pharaoh's lean kine[54]
       are to be loved. No, my good lord; banish Peto, banish Bardolph,
       banish Poins: but for sweet Jack Falstaff, kind Jack Falstaff, true Jack
       Falstaff, valiant Jack Falstaff, and therefore more valiant, being, as
       he is, old Jack Falstaff, banish not him thy Harry's company, banish
       not him thy Harry's company: banish plump Jack, and banish all
       the world.
PRINCE.   I do, I will.   [A *knocking heard.*
                           [*Exeunt Hostess, Francis, and Bardolph.*

                        Re-enter BARDOLPH, *running*

BARD.   O, my lord, my lord! the sheriff with a most monstrous watch is
        at the door.
FAL.   Out, ye rogue! Play out the play: I have much to say in the behalf
       of that Falstaff.

                        Re-enter the Hostess

HOST.   O Jesu, my lord, my lord! —
PRINCE.   Heigh, heigh! the devil rides upon a fiddlestick:[55] what's the
          matter?
HOST.   The sheriff and all the watch are at the door: they are come to
        search the house. Shall I let them in?
FAL.   Dost thou hear, Hal? never call a true piece of gold a counterfeit:
       thou art essentially mad, without seeming so.[56]
PRINCE.   And thou a natural coward, without instinct.
FAL.   I deny your major:[57] if you will deny the sheriff, so; if not, let him
       enter: if I become not a cart[58] as well as another man, a plague on
       my bringing up! I hope I shall as soon be strangled with a halter as
       another.

---

54. *kine*] cattle. See Exodus 9:3–7.
55. *the devil . . . fiddlestick*] a proverbial phrase; meaning, here's a to-do about nothing.
56. *thou art essentially mad, without seeming so*] you are really mad (by the way you have
    been taking me off): there is no need to pretend to be a lunatic.
57. *major*] the major proposition. "Major" being pronounced "mayor" by Falstaff makes the
    punning allusion to "the sheriff" clear.
58. *become not a cart*] look not well in the hangman's cart (which takes the criminal to the
    scaffold).

PRINCE. Go, hide thee behind the arras:[59] the rest walk up above. Now, my masters, for a true face and good conscience.

FAL. Both which I have had; but their date is out, and therefore I'll hide me.

PRINCE. Call in the sheriff. [*Exeunt all except the Prince and Peto.*

Enter Sheriff *and the* Carrier

Now, master sheriff, what is your will with me?

SHER. First, pardon me, my lord. A hue and cry
Hath follow'd certain men unto this house.

PRINCE. What men?

SHER. One of them is well known, my gracious lord,
A gross fat man.

CAR.   As fat as butter.

PRINCE. The man, I do assure you, is not here;
For I myself at this time have employ'd him.
And, sheriff, I will engage my word to thee
That I will, by to-morrow dinner-time,
Send him to answer thee, or any man,
For any thing he shall be charged withal:
And so let me entreat you leave the house.

SHER. I will, my lord. There are two gentlemen
Have in this robbery lost three hundred marks.

PRINCE. It may be so: if he have robb'd these men,
He shall be answerable; and so farewell.

SHER. Good night, my noble lord.

PRINCE. I think it is good morrow, is it not?

SHER. Indeed, my lord, I think it be two o'clock.
          [*Exeunt Sheriff and Carrier.*

PRINCE. This oily rascal is known as well as Paul's.[60]
Go, call him forth.

PETO. Falstaff! — Fast asleep behind the arras, and snorting like a horse.

PRINCE. Hark, how hard he fetches breath. Search his pockets. [*He searcheth his pockets, and findeth certain papers.*] What hast thou found?

PETO. Nothing but papers, my lord.

PRINCE. Let's see what they be: read them.

PETO. [*reads*] Item, A capon, . . . 2s. 2d.
          Item, Sauce, . . . 4d.
          Item, Sack, two gallons, . . . 5s. 8d.

59. *arras*] tapestry hanging at some distance from the walls.
60. *Paul's*] St. Paul's Cathedral.

    Item, Anchovies and sack after supper, . . . 2s. 6d.

    Item, Bread, . . . ob.[61]

PRINCE. O monstrous! but one half-pennyworth of bread to this intol-
erable deal of sack! What there is else, keep close; we'll read it at
more advantage; there let him sleep till day. I'll to the court in the
morning. We must all to the wars, and thy place shall be honourable. I'll procure this fat rogue a charge of foot;[62] and I know his
death will be a march of twelve-score.[63] The money shall be paid
back again with advantage. Be with me betimes in the morning;
and so, good morrow, Peto.

PETO. Good morrow, good my lord.   [*Exeunt.*

---

61. *ob.*] abbreviation of the Latin "obolus," commonly used in England as a symbol for a
    half-penny.

62. *a charge of foot*] command of a company of foot-soldiers.

63. *his death . . . twelve-score*] he will die if he march a distance of twelve-score yards.

ACT III.

SCENE I. *Bangor. The Archdeacon's House.*

Enter HOTSPUR, WORCESTER, MORTIMER, *and* GLENDOWER

MORTIMER.   These promises are fair, the parties sure,
    And our induction[1] full of prosperous hope.
HOT.   Lord Mortimer, and cousin Glendower,
    Will you sit down?
    And uncle Worcester: a plague upon it!
    I have forgot the map.
GLEND.   No, here it is.
    Sit, cousin Percy; sit, good cousin Hotspur.
    For by that name as oft as Lancaster
    Doth speak of you, his cheek looks pale, and with
    A rising sigh he wisheth you in heaven.
HOT.   And you in hell, as oft as he hears Owen Glendower spoke of.
GLEND.   I cannot blame him: at my nativity
    The front of heaven was full of fiery shapes,
    Of burning cressets;[2] and at my birth
    The frame and huge foundation of the earth
    Shaked like a coward.
HOT.   Why, so it would have done at the same season, if your mother's
    cat had but kittened, though yourself had never been born.
GLEND.   I say the earth did shake when I was born.
HOT.   And I say the earth was not of my mind,
    If you suppose as fearing you it shook.
GLEND.   The heavens were all on fire, the earth did tremble.
HOT.   O, then the earth shook to see the heavens on fire,
    And not in fear of your nativity.

---

1. *induction*] opening scene, first move.
2. *cressets*] beacons.

Diseased nature oftentimes breaks forth
In strange eruptions; oft the teeming earth
Is with a kind of colic pinch'd and vex'd
By the imprisoning of unruly wind
Within her womb; which, for enlargement striving,
Shakes the old beldam[3] earth and topples down
Steeples and moss-grown towers. At your birth
Our grandam earth, having this distemperature,
In passion shook.
GLEND.　　　　　Cousin, of many men
　I do not bear these crossings. Give me leave
　To tell you once again that at my birth
　The front of heaven was full of fiery shapes,
　The goats ran from the mountains, and the herds
　Were strangely clamorous to the frighted fields.
　These signs have mark'd me extraordinary;
　And all the courses of my life do show
　I am not in the roll of common men.
　Where is he living, clipp'd in with the sea
　That chides the banks of England, Scotland, Wales,
　Which calls me pupil, or hath read to me?
　And bring him out that is but woman's son
　Can trace me in the tedious ways of art,
　And hold me pace in deep experiments.[4]
HOT.　I think there's no man speaks better Welsh, I'll to dinner.
MORT.　Peace, cousin Percy; you will make him mad.
GLEND.　I can call spirits from the vasty deep.
HOT.　Why, so can I, or so can any man;
　But will they come when you do call for them?
GLEND.　Why, I can teach you, cousin, to command
　The devil.
HOT.　And I can teach thee, coz, to shame the devil
　By telling truth: tell truth, and shame the devil.
　If thou have power to raise him, bring him hither,
　And I'll be sworn I have power to shame him hence.
　O, while you live, tell truth, and shame the devil!
MORT.　Come, come, no more of this unprofitable chat.
GLEND.　Three times hath Henry Bolingbroke made head
　Against my power; thrice from the banks of Wye
　And sandy-bottom'd Severn have I sent him

3. *beldam*] grandmother.
4. *And bring him out . . . experiments*] And produce any one who, being mortal, can follow me in tedious ways of learning and keep pace with me in deep experiments.

Bootless home and weather-beaten back.
HOT.   Home without boots, and in foul weather too!
How 'scapes he agues,[5] in the devil's name?
GLEND.   Come, here's the map: shall we divide our right
According to our threefold order ta'en?[6]
MORT.   The archdeacon hath divided it
Into three limits very equally:
England, from Trent and Severn hitherto,
By south and east is to my part assign'd:
All westward, Wales beyond the Severn shore,
And all the fertile land within that bound,
To Owen Glendower: and, dear coz, to you
The remnant northward, lying off from Trent.
And our indentures tripartite are drawn;
Which being sealed interchangeably,
A business that this night may execute,
To-morrow, cousin Percy, you and I
And my good Lord of Worcester will set forth
To meet your father and the Scottish power,
As is appointed us, at Shrewsbury.
My father Glendower is not ready yet,
Nor shall we need his help these fourteen days.
Within that space you may have drawn together
Your tenants, friends, and neighbouring gentlemen.
GLEND.   A shorter time shall send me to you, lords:
And in my conduct shall your ladies come;
From whom you now must steal and take no leave,
For there will be a world of water shed
Upon the parting of your wives and you.
HOT.   Methinks my moiety, north from Burton here,
In quantity equals not one of yours:
See how this river comes me cranking in,[7]
And cuts me from the best of all my land
A huge half-moon, a monstrous cantle[8] out,
I'll have the current in this place damm'd up;
And here the smug and silver Trent shall run
In a new channel, fair and evenly;
It shall not wind with such a deep indent,
To rob me of so rich a bottom here.

5. *How 'scapes he agues*] How does he avoid catching cold?
6. *our threefold order ta'en*] our agreement to divide the country in three parts.
7. *comes me cranking in*] comes meandering and twisting about my land.
8. *cantle*] corner, bit (of anything).

GLEND. Not wind? it shall, it must; you see it doth.
MORT. Yea, but
    Mark how he bears his course, and runs me up
    With like advantage on the other side;
    Gelding the opposed continent as much
    As on the other side it takes from you.
WOR. Yea, but a little charge will trench him here,
    And on this north side win this cape of land;
    And then he runs straight and even.
HOT. I'll have it so: a little charge will do it.
GLEND. I'll not have it alter'd.
HOT.   Will not you?
GLEND. No, nor you shall not.
HOT.   Who shall say me nay?
GLEND. Why, that will I.
HOT. Let me not understand you, then; speak it in Welsh.
GLEND. I can speak English, lord, as well as you;
    For I was train'd up in the English court;
    Where, being but young, I framed to the harp
    Many an English ditty lovely well,
    And gave the tongue a helpful ornament,
    A virtue that was never seen in you.
HOT. Marry,
    And I am glad of it with all my heart:
    I had rather be a kitten and cry mew
    Than one of these same metre ballad-mongers;
    I had rather hear a brazen canstick[9] turn'd,
    Or a dry wheel grate on the axle-tree;
    And that would set my teeth nothing on edge,
    Nothing so much as mincing poetry:
    'Tis like the forced gait of a shuffling nag.
GLEND. Come, you shall have Trent turn'd.
HOT. I do not care: I'll give thrice so much land
    To any well-deserving friend;
    But in the way of bargain, mark ye me,
    I'll cavil on[10] the ninth part of a hair.
    Are the indentures drawn? shall we be gone?
GLEND. The moon shines fair; you may away by night:
    I'll haste the writer,[11] and withal

---

  9. *canstick*] candlestick.
 10. *cavil on*] haggle over.
 11. *the writer*] the copyist of the agreements.

Break with[12] your wives of your departure hence:
I am afraid my daughter will run mad,
So much she doteth on her Mortimer.   [*Exit.*
MORT.   Fie, cousin Percy! how you cross my father!
HOT.   I cannot choose: sometime he angers me
With telling me of the moldwarp and the ant,
Of the dreamer Merlin and his prophecies,
And of a dragon and a finless fish,
A clip-wing'd griffin and a moulten raven,
A couching lion and a ramping[13] cat,[14]
And such a deal of skimble-skamble stuff[15]
As puts me from my faith. I tell you what, —
He held me last night at least nine hours
In reckoning up the several devils' names
That were his lackeys: I cried "hum," and "well, go to,"
But mark'd him not a word. O, he is as tedious
As a tired horse, a railing wife;
Worse than a smoky house: I had rather live
With cheese and garlic in a windmill, far,
Than feed on cates[16] and have him talk to me
In any summer-house in Christendom.
MORT.   In faith, he is a worthy gentleman,
Exceedingly well read, and profited
In strange concealments;[17] valiant as a lion,
And wondrous affable, and as bountiful
As mines of India. Shall I tell you, cousin?
He holds your temper in a high respect,
And curbs himself even of his natural scope
When you come 'cross his humour; faith, he does:
I warrant you, that man is not alive
Might so have tempted him as you have done,
Without the taste of danger and reproof:
But do not use it oft, let me entreat you.
WOR.   In faith, my lord, you are too wilful-blame;[18]

---

12. *Break with*] Communicate to.
13. *couching . . . ramping*] lying down . . . rearing; heraldic terms.
14. *of the moldwarp . . . cat*] Hotspur makes impatient and scornfully inexact reference to an
    old prophecy attributed to Merlin in which Glendower put faith, to the effect that Henry
    IV, who was likened by Merlin to "a moldwarp" (*i.e.*, a mole), should lose his realm to a
    band of three assailants, viz., a dragon, a lion, and a wolf.
15. *skimble-skamble stuff*] random nonsense.
16. *cates*] dainties, delicacies.
17. *profited . . . concealments*] skilled in wonderful secrets.
18. *wilful-blame*] wilfully to blame.

And since your coming hither have done enough
To put him quite beside his patience.
You must needs learn, lord, to amend this fault:
Though sometimes it show greatness, courage, blood, —
And that's the dearest grace it renders you, —
Yet oftentimes it doth present harsh rage,
Defect of manners, want of government,
Pride, haughtiness, opinion and disdain:
The least of which haunting a nobleman
Loseth men's hearts, and leaves behind a stain
Upon the beauty of all parts besides,
Beguiling them of commendation.[19]

HOT.   Well, I am school'd: good manners be your speed!
Here come our wives, and let us take our leave.

Re-enter GLENDOWER *with the* ladies

MORT.   This is the deadly spite that angers me;
My wife can speak no English, I no Welsh.

GLEND.   My daughter weeps: she will not part with you;
She'll be a soldier too, she'll to the wars.

MORT.   Good father, tell her that she and my aunt Percy
Shall follow in your conduct speedily.

*[Glendower speaks to her in Welsh, and she answers
him in the same.*

GLEND.   She is desperate here; a peevish self-will'd harlotry, one that no
persuasion can do good upon.   *[The lady speaks in Welsh.*

MORT.   I understand thy looks: that pretty Welsh
Which thou pour'st down from these swelling heavens[20]
I am too perfect in; and, but for shame,
In such a parley should I answer thee.

[The lady speaks again in Welsh.

I understand thy kisses and thou mine,
And that's a feeling disputation:[21]
But I will never be a truant, love,
Till I have learn'd thy language; for thy tongue
Makes Welsh as sweet as ditties highly penn'd,
Sung by a fair queen in a summer's bower,
With ravishing division,[22] to her lute.

GLEND.   Nay, if you melt, then will she run mad.

[The lady speaks again in Welsh.

---

19. *Beguiling . . . commendation*] Cheating them of the praise due them.
20. *heavens*] i.e., eyes.
21. *a feeling disputation*] a theme of sensibility.
22. *division*] variations on a melody.

MORT.   O, I am ignorance itself in this!
GLEND.   She bids you on the wanton[23] rushes lay you down
   And rest your gentle head upon her lap,
   And she will sing the song that pleaseth you,
   And on your eyelids crown the god of sleep,
   Charming your blood with pleasing heaviness,
   Making such difference 'twixt wake and sleep
   As is the difference betwixt day and night
   The hour before the heavenly-harness'd team
   Begins his golden progress in the east.
MORT.   With all my heart I'll sit and hear her sing:
   By that time will our book, I think, be drawn.[24]
GLEND.   Do so;
   And those musicians that shall play to you
   Hang in the air a thousand leagues from hence,
   And straight they shall be here: sit, and attend.
HOT.   Come, Kate, thou art perfect in lying down: come, quick, quick,
   that I may lay my head in thy lap.
LADY P.   Go, ye giddy goose.   [*The music plays.*
HOT.   Now I perceive the devil understands Welsh;
   And 'tis no marvel he is so humorous.[25]
   By 'r lady, he is a good musician.
LADY P.   Then should you be nothing but musical, for you are altogether
   governed by humours. Lie still, ye thief, and hear the lady sing in
   Welsh.
HOT.   I had rather hear Lady, my brach,[26] howl in Irish.
LADY P.   Wouldst thou have thy head broken?
HOT.   No.
LADY P.   Then be still.
HOT.   Neither; 'tis a woman's fault.
LADY P.   Now God help thee!
HOT.   To the Welsh lady's bed.
LADY P.   What's that?
HOT.   Peace! she sings.   [*Here the lady sings a Welsh song.*
HOT.   Come, Kate, I'll have your song too.
LADY P.   Not mine, in good sooth.
HOT.   Not yours, in good sooth! Heart! you swear like a comfit-maker's[27]

---

23. *wanton*] soft.
24. *our book . . . be drawn*] our agreements be drawn out.
25. *humorous*] capricious.
26. *brach*] bitch-hound.
27. *comfit-maker's*] confectioner's.

wife. "Not you, in good sooth," and "as true as I live," and "as God
shall mend me," and "as sure as day,"
And givest such sarcenet[28] surety for thy oaths,
As if thou never walk'st further than Finsbury.[29]
Swear me, Kate, like a lady as thou art,
A good mouth-filling oath, and leave "in sooth,"
And such protest of pepper-gingerbread,
To velvet-guards[30] and Sunday-citizens.
Come, sing.
LADY P.   I will not sing.
HOT.   'Tis the next way to turn tailor,[31] or be red-breast teacher. An the
indentures be drawn, I'll away within these two hours; and so, come
in when ye will.   [*Exit.*
GLEND.   Come, come, Lord Mortimer; you are as slow
As hot Lord Percy is on fire to go.
By this our book is drawn; we'll but seal,
And then to horse immediately.
MORT.   With all my heart.   [*Exeunt.*

SCENE II.   *London. The Palace.*

Enter the KING, PRINCE OF WALES, *and others*

KING.   Lords, give us leave;[1] the Prince of Wales and I
Must have some private conference: but be near at hand,
For we shall presently have need of you.   [*Exeunt Lords.*
I know not whether God will have it so,
For some displeasing service I have done,
That, in his secret doom,[2] out of my blood
He'll breed revengement and a scourge for me;

---

28. *sarcenet*] soft, like the silken material known by that name.
29. *Finsbury*] a district where London citizens were wont to promenade.
30. *velvet-guards*] weavers of clothing trimmed with velvet.
31. *turn tailor*] tailors were noted for their singing.

---

1. *give us leave*] withdraw.
2. *doom*] judgment.

    But thou dost in thy passages of life
    Make me believe that thou art only mark'd
    For the hot vengeance and the rod of heaven
    To punish my mistreadings. Tell me else,
    Could such inordinate and low desires,
    Such poor, such bare, such lewd, such mean attempts,
    Such barren pleasures, rude society,
    As thou art match'd withal and grafted to,
    Accompany the greatness of thy blood,
    And hold their level with thy princely heart?
PRINCE.   So please your majesty, I would I could
    Quit all offences with as clear excuse
    As well as I am doubtless I can purge
    Myself of many I am charged withal:
    Yet such extenuation let me beg,
    As, in reproof of many tales devised,
    Which oft the ear of greatness needs must hear,
    By smiling pick-thanks[3] and base newsmongers,
    I may, for some things true, wherein my youth
    Hath faulty wander'd and irregular,
    Find pardon on my true submission.
KING.   God pardon thee! yet let me wonder, Harry,
    At thy affections, which do hold a wing
    Quite from the flight of all thy ancestors.
    Thy place in council thou hast rudely lost,
    Which by thy younger brother is supplied,
    And art almost an alien to the hearts
    Of all the court and princes of my blood:
    The hope and expectation of thy time
    Is ruin'd, and the soul of every man
    Prophetically doth forethink thy fall.
    Had I so lavish of my presence been,
    So common-hackney'd in the eyes of men,
    So stale and cheap to vulgar company,
    Opinion, that did help me to the crown,
    Had still kept loyal to possession,[4]
    And left me in reputeless banishment,
    A fellow of no mark nor likelihood.
    By being seldom seen, I could not stir
    But like a comet I was wonder'd at;
    That men would tell their children "This is he;"

---

3. *pick-thanks*] parasites, flatterers.
4. *possession*] i.e., to the sovereignty of Richard II.

Others would say "Where, which is Bolingbroke?"
And then I stole all courtesy from heaven,[5]
And dress'd myself in such humility
That I did pluck allegiance from men's hearts,
Loud shouts and salutations from their mouths,
Even in the presence of the crowned king.
Thus did I keep my person fresh and new;
My presence, like a robe pontifical
Ne'er seen but wonder'd at: and so my state,
Seldom but sumptuous, showed like a feast,
And wan by rareness such solemnity.
The skipping[6] king, he ambled up and down,
With shallow jesters and rash bavin[7] wits,
Soon kindled and soon burnt; carded[8] his state,
Mingled his royalty with capering fools,
Had his great name profaned with their scorns,
And gave his countenance, against his name,[9]
To laugh at gibing boys, and stand the push[10]
Of every beardless vain comparative,
Grew a companion to the common streets,
Enfeoff'd[11] himself to popularity;
That, being daily swallow'd by men's eyes,
They surfeited with honey and began
To loathe the taste of sweetness, whereof a little
More than a little is by much too much.
So when he had occasion to be seen,
He was but as the cuckoo is in June,
Heard, not regarded; seen, but with such eyes
As, sick and blunted with community,[12]
Afford no extraordinary gaze,
Such as is bent on sun-like majesty
When it shines seldom in admiring eyes;
But rather drowsed and hung their eyelids down,
Slept in his face and render'd such aspect
As cloudy[13] men use to their adversaries,

---

5. *stole . . . heaven*] assumed a manner of the utmost courtesy.
6. *skipping*] flighty, wanton.
7. *bavin*] brushwood, "soon kindled and soon burnt."
8. *carded*] debased.
9. *name*] dignity.
10. *push*] insolence.
11. *Enfeoff'd*] Gave himself up to.
12. *community*] familiarity.
13. *cloudy*] sullen, morose.

Being with his presence glutted, gorged and full.
And in that very line, Harry, standest thou;
For thou hast lost thy princely privilege
With vile participation:[14] not an eye
But is a-weary of thy common sight,
Save mine, which hath desired to see thee more;
Which now doth that I would not have it do,
Make blind itself with foolish tenderness.

PRINCE.   I shall hereafter, my thrice gracious lord,
Be more myself.

KING.   For all the world
As thou art to this hour was Richard then
When I from France set foot at Ravenspurgh,
And even as I was then is Percy now.
Now, by my sceptre and my soul to boot,
He hath more worthy interest[15] to the state
Than thou the shadow of succession;[16]
For of no right, nor colour like to right,
He doth fill fields with harness[17] in the realm,
Turns head against the lion's armed jaws,
And, being no more in debt to years than thou,
Leads ancient lords and reverend bishops on
To bloody battles and to bruising arms.
What never-dying honour hath he got
Against renowned Douglas! whose high deeds,
Whose hot incursions and great name in arms
Holds from all soldiers chief majority[18]
And military title capital[19]
Through all the kingdoms that acknowledge Christ:
Thrice hath this Hotspur, Mars in swathling[20] clothes,
This infant warrior, in his enterprizes
Discomfited great Douglas, ta'en him once,
Enlarged him and made a friend of him,
To fill the mouth of deep defiance up,
And shake the peace and safety of our throne.
And what say you to this? Percy, Northumberland,
The Archbishop's grace of York, Douglas, Mortimer,

---

14. *vile participation*] low companionship or society.
15. *interest*] claim, title.
16. *shadow of succession*] heir apparent.
17. *harness*] armor; here, armed warriors.
18. *majority*] preeminence.
19. *capital*] principal.
20. *swathling*] swaddling.

Capitulate[21] against us and are up.
But wherefore do I tell these news to thee?
Why, Harry, do I tell thee of my foes,
Which art my near'st and dearest enemy?
Thou that art like enough, through vassal fear
Base inclination and the start of spleen,[22]
To fight against me under Percy's pay,
To dog his heels and curtsy at his frowns,
To show how much thou art degenerate.

PRINCE.   Do not think so; you shall not find it so:
And God forgive them that so much have sway'd
Your majesty's good thoughts away from me!
I will redeem all this on Percy's head,
And in the closing of some glorious day
Be bold to tell you that I am your son;
When I will wear a garment all of blood,
And stain my favours in a bloody mask,
Which, wash'd away, shall scour my shame with it:
And that shall be the day, whene'er it lights,
That this same child of honour and renown,
This gallant Hotspur, this all-praised knight,
And your unthought-of Harry chance to meet.
For every honour sitting on his helm,
Would they were multitudes, and on my head
My shames redoubled! for the time will come,
That I shall make this northern youth exchange
His glorious deeds for my indignities.
Percy is but my factor, good my lord,
To engross up glorious deeds on my behalf;
And I will call him to so strict account,
That he shall render every glory up,
Yea, even the slightest worship of his time,
Or I will tear the reckoning from his heart.
This, in the name of God, I promise here:
The which if He be pleased I shall perform,
I do beseech your majesty may salve
The long-grown wounds of my intemperance:
If not, the end of life cancels all bands;
And I will die a hundred thousand deaths
Ere break the smallest parcel of this vow.

---

21. *Capitulate*] Form a league.
22. *start of spleen*] impulse of anger.

KING.   A hundred thousand rebels die in this:
Thou shalt have charge and sovereign trust herein.

Enter BLUNT

How now, good Blunt? thy looks are full of speed.
BLUNT.   So hath the business that I come to speak of.
Lord Mortimer of Scotland hath sent word
That Douglas and the English rebels met
The eleventh of this month at Shrewsbury:
A mighty and a fearful head they are,
If promises be kept on every hand,
As ever offer'd foul play in a state.
KING.   The Earl of Westmoreland set forth to-day;
With him my son, Lord John of Lancaster;
For this advertisement[23] is five days old:
On Wednesday next, Harry, you shall set forward;
On Thursday we ourselves will march: our meeting
Is Bridgenorth: and, Harry, you shall march
Through Gloucestershire; by which account,
Our business valued, some twelve days hence
Our general forces at Bridgenorth shall meet.
Our hands are full of business: let's away;
Advantage feeds him[24] fat, while men delay.   [*Exeunt.*

SCENE III.   *The Boar's-Head Tavern in Eastcheap.*

Enter FALSTAFF *and* BARDOLPH

FAL.   Bardolph, am I not fallen away vilely since this last action? do I
not bate? do I not dwindle? Why, my skin hangs about me like an
old lady's loose gown; I am withered like an old apple-john.[1] Well,
I'll repent, and that suddenly, while I am in some liking;[2] I shall be
out of heart shortly, and then I shall have no strength to repent. An
I have not forgotten what the inside of a church is made of, I am
a peppercorn, a brewer's horse:[3] the inside of a church! Company,
villanous company, hath been the spoil of me.

---

23. *advertisement*] intelligence, information.
24. *feeds him*] feeds himself, grows.

---

1. *apple-john*] apple, which kept long though the skin shrivelled quickly.
2. *in some liking*] in fairly good condition.
3. *brewer's horse*] a horse that is lank and bony.

BARD. Sir John, you are so fretful, you cannot live long.

FAL. Why, there is it: come sing me a bawdy song; make me merry. I was as virtuously given as a gentleman need to be; virtuous enough; swore little; diced not above seven times a week; went to a bawdy-house not above once in a quarter — of an hour; paid money that I borrowed, three or four times; lived well, and in good compass: and now I live out of all order, out of all compass.

BARD. Why, you are so fat, Sir John, that you must needs be out of all compass, out of all reasonable compass, Sir John.

FAL. Do thou amend thy face, and I'll amend my life: thou art our admiral, thou bearest the lantern in the poop, but 'tis in the nose of thee; thou art the Knight of the Burning Lamp.

BARD. Why, Sir John, my face does you no harm.

FAL. No, I'll be sworn; I make as good use of it as many a man doth of a Death's-head or a memento mori:[4] I never see thy face but I think upon hell-fire, and Dives[5] that lived in purple; for there he is in his robes, burning, burning. If thou wert any way given to virtue, I would swear by thy face; my oath should be, "By this fire, that's God's angel:"[6] but thou art altogether given over; and wert indeed, but for the light in thy face, the son of utter darkness. When thou rannest up Gadshill in the night to catch my horse, if I did not think thou hadst been an ignis fatuus[7] or a ball of wildfire, there's no purchase in money. O, thou art a perpetual triumph, an ever-lasting bonfire-light! Thou hast saved me a thousand marks in links and torches, walking with thee in the night betwixt tavern and tavern: but the sack that thou hast drunk me would have bought me lights as good cheap[8] at the dearest chandler's in Europe. I have maintained that salamander of yours with fire any time this two and thirty years; God reward me for it!

BARD. 'Sblood, I would my face were in your belly!

FAL. God-a-mercy! so should I be sure to be heart-burned.

Enter Hostess

How now, Dame Partlet[9] the hen! have you inquired yet who picked my pocket?

HOST. Why, Sir John, what do you think, Sir John? do you think I keep thieves in my house? I have searched, I have inquired, so has my

---

4. *memento mori*] a common term for a skull and crossbones.
5. *Dives*] the rich man in the parable (Luke 16:19).
6. *By . . . angel*] Cf. Exodus 3:2, Psalms 104:4, and Hebrews 1:7.
7. *an ignis fatuus*] a will o' the wisp.
8. *as good cheap*] quite as cheaply.
9. *Dame Partlet*] The name of the hen in the medieval story of Reynard the Fox.

husband, man by man, boy by boy, servant by servant: the tithe of a hair was never lost in my house before.

FAL.. Ye lie, hostess: Bardolph was shaved, and lost many a hair; and I'll be sworn my pocket was picked. Go to, you are a woman, go.

HOST. Who, I? no; I defy thee: God's light, I was never called so in mine own house before.

FAL.. Go to, I know you well enough.

HOST. No, Sir John; you do not know me, Sir John. I know you, Sir John: you owe me money, Sir John; and now you pick a quarrel to beguile me of it: I bought you a dozen of shirts to your back.

FAL.. Dowlas,[10] filthy dowlas: I have given them away to bakers' wives, and they have made bolters[11] of them.

HOST. Now, as I am a true woman, holland[12] of eight shillings an ell. You owe money here besides, Sir John, for your diet and by-drinkings, and money lent you, four and twenty pound.

FAL.. He had his part of it; let him pay.

HOST. He? alas, he is poor: he hath nothing.

FAL.. How! poor? look upon his face; what call you rich? let them coin his nose, let them coin his cheeks: I'll not pay a denier.[13] What, will you make a younker[14] of me? shall I not take mine ease in mine inn but I shall have my pocket picked? I have lost a seal-ring of my grandfather's worth forty mark.

HOST. O Jesu, I have heard the prince tell him, I know not how oft, that that ring was copper!

FAL.. How! the prince is a Jack, a sneak-cup:[15] 'sblood, and he were here, I would cudgel him like a dog, if he would say so.

Enter the PRINCE *and* PETO, *marching, and* FALSTAFF *meets them playing on his truncheon like a fife*

How now, lad! is the wind in that door, i' faith? must we all march?

BARD. Yea, two and two, Newgate[16] fashion.

HOST. My lord, I pray you, hear me.

PRINCE. What sayest thou, Mistress Quickly? How doth thy husband? I love him well; he is an honest man.

HOST. Good my lord, hear me.

FAL.. Prithee, let her alone, and list to me.

PRINCE. What sayest thou, Jack?

---

10. *Dowlas*] The coarsest kind of linen.
11. *bolters*] cloth or hair sieves for sifting meal or flour.
12. *holland*] fine linen.
13. *a denier*] a penny, a stiver, from Latin "denarius."
14. *younker*] greenhorn.
15. *sneak-cup*] one who dodges liquor, who slily avoids drinking his share.
16. *Newgate*] a London prison. Prisoners were marched there in pairs.

FAL. The other night I fell asleep here behind the arras, and had my pocket picked: this house is turned bawdy-house; they pick pockets.

PRINCE. What didst thou lose, Jack?

FAL. Wilt thou believe me, Hal? three or four bonds of forty pound a-piece, and a seal-ring of my grandfather's.

PRINCE. A trifle, some eight-penny matter.

HOST. So I told him, my lord; and I said I heard your grace say so: and, my lord, he speaks most vilely of you, like a foul-mouthed man as he is; and said he would cudgel you.

PRINCE. What! he did not?

HOST. There's neither faith, truth, nor womanhood in me else.

FAL. There's no more faith in thee than in a stewed prune;[17] nor no more truth in thee than in a drawn fox;[18] and for womanhood, Maid Marian may be the deputy's wife of the ward to thee. Go, you thing, go.

HOST. Say, what thing? what thing?

FAL. What thing! why, a thing to thank God on.

HOST. I am no thing to thank God on, I would thou shouldst know it; I am an honest man's wife: and, setting thy knighthood aside, thou art a knave to call me so.

FAL. Setting thy womanhood aside, thou art a beast to say otherwise.

HOST. Say, what beast, thou knave, thou?

FAL. What beast! why, an otter.

PRINCE. An otter, Sir John! why an otter?

FAL. Why, she's neither fish nor flesh; a man knows not where to have her.

HOST. Thou art an unjust man in saying so: thou or any man knows where to have me, thou knave, thou!

PRINCE. Thou sayest true, hostess; and he slanders thee most grossly.

HOST. So he doth you, my lord; and said this other day you ought[19] him a thousand pound.

PRINCE. Sirrah, do I owe you a thousand pound?

FAL. A thousand pound, Hal! a million: thy love is worth a million: thou owest me thy love.

HOST. Nay, my lord, he called you Jack, and said he would cudgel you.

FAL. Did I, Bardolph?

BARD. Indeed, Sir John, you said so.

FAL. Yea, if he said my ring was copper.

PRINCE. I say 'tis copper: darest thou be as good as thy word now?

---

17. *a stewed prune*] commonly eaten in bawdy houses.

18. *a drawn fox*] a fox drawn from cover, and wily in getting back.

19. *ought*] owed.

FAL. Why, Hal, thou knowest, as thou art but man, I dare: but as thou art prince, I fear thee as I fear the roaring of the lion's whelp.

PRINCE. And why not as the lion?

FAL. The king himself is to be feared as the lion; dost thou think I'll fear thee as I fear thy father? nay, and I do, I pray God my girdle break.

PRINCE. O, if it should, how would thy guts fall about thy knees! But, sirrah, there's no room for faith, truth, nor honesty in this bosom of thine; it is all filled up with guts and midriff. Charge an honest woman with picking thy pocket! why, thou whoreson, impudent, embossed[20] rascal, if there were anything in thy pocket but tavern-reckonings, memorandums of bawdy-houses, and one poor penny-worth of sugar-candy to make thee long-winded, if thy pocket were enriched with any other injuries but these, I am a villain: and yet you will stand to it; you will not pocket up wrong:[21] art thou not ashamed?

FAL. Dost thou hear, Hal? thou knowest in the state of innocency Adam fell; and what should poor Jack Falstaff do in the days of villany? Thou seest I have more flesh than another man; and therefore more frailty. You confess then, you picked my pocket?

PRINCE. It appears so by the story.

FAL. Hostess, I forgive thee: go, make ready breakfast; love thy husband, look to thy servants, cherish thy guests: thou shalt find me tractable to any honest reason: thou seest I am pacified still. Nay, prithee, be gone. [*Exit Hostess.*] Now, Hal, to the news at court: for the robbery, lad, how is that answered?

PRINCE. O, my sweet beef, I must still be good angel to thee: the money is paid back again.

FAL. O, I do not like that paying back; 'tis a double labour.

PRINCE. I am good friends with my father, and may do any thing.

FAL. Rob me the exchequer the first thing thou doest, and do it with unwashed hands[22] too.

BARD. Do, my lord.

PRINCE. I have procured thee, Jack, a charge of foot.

FAL. I would it had been of horse. Where shall I find one that can steal well? O for a fine thief, of the age of two and twenty or thereabouts! I am heinously unprovided. Well, God be thanked for these rebels, they offend none but the virtuous: I laud them, I praise them.

PRINCE. Bardolph!

BARD. My lord?

---

20. *embossed*] swollen.
21. *pocket up wrong*] bear injury tamely, without resentment.
22. *with unwashed hands*] at once, without waiting (to wash your hands).

PRINCE. Go bear this letter to Lord John of Lancaster, to my brother
      John; this to my Lord of Westmoreland. [*Exit Bardolph.*] Go, Peto,
      to horse, to horse; for thou and I have thirty miles to ride yet ere
      dinner time. [*Exit Peto.*] Jack, meet me to-morrow in the Temple
      hall at two o'clock in the afternoon.
      There shalt thou know thy charge, and there receive
      Money and order for their furniture.[23]
      The land is burning; Percy stands on high;
      And either we or they must lower lie.   [*Exit.*
FAL.   Rare words! brave world! Hostess, my breakfast, come!
      O, I could wish this tavern were my drum![24]   [*Exit.*

---

23. *furniture*] equipment.
24. *my drum*] my headquarters, my rendezvous.

ACT IV.

SCENE I. *The Rebel Camp near Shrewsbury.*

Enter HOTSPUR, WORCESTER, *and* DOUGLAS

HOTSPUR.   Well said, my noble Scot: if speaking truth
In this fine age were not thought flattery,
Such attribution[1] should the Douglas have,
As not a soldier of this season's stamp
Should go so general current through the world.
By God, I cannot flatter; I do defy
The tongues of soothers;[2] but a braver place
In my heart's love hath no man than yourself:
Nay, task me to my word; approve me,[3] lord.

DOUG.   Thou art the king of honour:
No man so potent breathes upon the ground
But I will beard[4] him.

HOT.   Do so, and 'tis well.

Enter a Messenger *with letters*

What letters hast thou there? — I can but thank you.

MESS.   These letters come from your father.

HOT.   Letters from him! why comes he not himself?

MESS.   He cannot come, my lord; he is grievous sick.

HOT.   'Zounds! how has he the leisure to be sick
In such a justling[5] time? Who leads his power?
Under whose government come they along?

MESS.   His letters bear his mind, not I, my lord.

---

1. *attribution*] credit.
2. *defy . . . soothers*] disdain flattering tongues.
3. *task . . . approve me*] put my word to the proof, try me.
4. *beard*] defy.
5. *justling*] jostling.

60

WOR.   I prithee, tell me, doth he keep his bed?
MESS.   He did, my lord, four days ere I set forth;
    And at the time of my departure thence
    He was much fear'd by his physicians.
WOR.   I would the state of time had first been whole,
    Ere he by sickness had been visited:
    His health was never better worth than now.
HOT.   Sick now! droop now! this sickness doth infect
    The very life-blood of our enterprise;
    'Tis catching hither, even to our camp.
    He writes me here, that inward sickness —
    And that his friends by deputation could not
    So soon be drawn, nor did he think it meet
    To lay so dangerous and dear a trust
    On any soul removed but on his own.
    Yet doth he give us bold advertisement,[6]
    That with our small conjunction we should on,
    To see how fortune is disposed to us;
    For, as he writes, there is no quailing now,
    Because the king is certainly possess'd
    Of all our purposes. What say you to it?
WOR.   Your father's sickness is a maim to us.
HOT.   A perilous gash, a very limb lopp'd off:
    And yet, in faith, it is not; his present want
    Seems more than we shall find it: were it good
    To set the exact wealth of all our states
    All at one cast? to set so rich a main[7]
    On the nice hazard of one doubtful hour?
    It were not good; for therein should we read
    The very bottom and the soul of hope,
    The very list, the very utmost bound
    Of all our fortunes.
DOUG.   Faith, and so we should;
    Where now remains a sweet reversion:[8]
    We may boldly spend upon the hope of what
    Is to come in:
    A comfort of retirement lives in this.
HOT.   A rendezvous, a home to fly unto,
    If that the devil and mischance look big
    Upon the maidenhead of our affairs.

---

6. *advertisement*] admonition.
7. *set so rich a main*] lay so large a stake.
8. *sweet reversion*] some hope in reserve.

WOR.　But yet I would your father had been here.
　　　The quality and hair[9] of our attempt
　　　Brooks no division: it will be thought
　　　By some, that know not why he is away,
　　　That wisdom, loyalty and mere dislike
　　　Of our proceedings kept the earl from hence:
　　　And think how such an apprehension
　　　May turn the tide of fearful faction,
　　　And breed a kind of question in our cause;
　　　For well you know we of the offering side[10]
　　　Must keep aloof from strict arbitrement,[11]
　　　And stop all sight-holes, every loop from whence
　　　The eye of reason may pry in upon us:
　　　This absence of your father's draws a curtain,
　　　That shows the ignorant a kind of fear
　　　Before not dreamt of.
HOT.　　　　　　　　　You strain too far.
　　　I rather of his absence make this use:
　　　It lends a lustre and more great opinion,
　　　A larger dare to our great enterprise,
　　　Than if the earl were here; for men must think,
　　　If we without his help can make a head
　　　To push against a kingdom, with his help
　　　We shall o'erturn it topsy-turvy down.
　　　Yet all goes well, yet all our joints are whole.
DOUG.　As heart can think: there is not such a word
　　　Spoke of in Scotland as this term of fear.

Enter SIR RICHARD VERNON

HOT.　My cousin Vernon! welcome, by my soul.
VER.　Pray God my news be worth a welcome, lord.
　　　The Earl of Westmoreland, seven thousand strong,
　　　Is marching hitherwards; with him Prince John.
HOT.　No harm: what more?
VER.　　　　　　　　And further, I have learn'd,
　　　The king himself in person is set forth,
　　　Or hitherwards intended speedily,
　　　With strong and mighty preparation.
HOT.　He shall be welcome too. Where is his son,
　　　The nimble-footed madcap Prince of Wales,

---

　　9. *hair*] complexion, character.
　10. *the offering side*] the attacking party.
　11. *arbitrement*] judicial inquiry.

And his comrades, that daff'd[12] the world aside,
And bid it pass?
VER.   All furnish'd, all in arms;
All plumed like estridges that with the wind
Baited[13] like eagles having lately bathed;
Glittering in golden coats, like images;[14]
As full of spirit as the month of May,
And gorgeous as the sun at midsummer;
Wanton as youthful goats, wild as young bulls.
I saw young Harry, with his beaver[15] on,
His cuisses[16] on his thighs, gallantly arm'd,
Rise from the ground like feather'd Mercury,
And vaulted with such ease into his seat,
As if an angel dropp'd down from the clouds,
To turn and wind a fiery Pegasus,
And witch the world with noble horsemanship.
HOT.   No more, no more: worse than the sun in March,
This praise doth nourish agues. Let them come;
They come like sacrifices in their trim,[17]
And to the fire-eyed maid of smoky war[18]
All hot and bleeding will we offer them:
The mailed Mars shall on his altar sit
Up to the ears in blood. I am on fire
To hear this rich reprisal is so nigh
And yet not ours. Come, let me taste[19] my horse,
Who is to bear me like a thunderbolt
Against the bosom of the Prince of Wales:
Harry to Harry shall, not horse to horse,
Meet and ne'er part till one drop down a corse.
O that Glendower were come!
VER.   There is more news:
I learn'd in Worcester, as I rode along,
He cannot draw his power this fourteen days.
DOUG.   That's the worst tidings that I hear of yet.
WOR.   Ay, by my faith, that bears a frosty sound.
HOT.   What may the king's whole battle reach unto?

---

12. *daff'd*] tossed contemptuously.
13. *Baited*] This should probably read "bated," flapped their wings.
14. *images*] gaudily painted saints' images.
15. *beaver*] visor of the helmet; here also the helmet itself.
16. *cuisses*] a French word for leg or thigh armour.
17. *trim*] fine apparel, trappings.
18. *maid of smoky war*] the goddess Bellona.
19. *taste*] test, try.

VER.   To thirty thousand.
HOT.   Forty let it be:
My father and Glendower being both away,
The powers of us may serve so great a day.
Come, let us take a muster speedily:
Doomsday is near; die all, die merrily.
DOUG.   Talk not of dying: I am out of fear
Of death or death's hand for this one half year.   [*Exeunt.*

SCENE II.   *A Public Road near Coventry.*

Enter FALSTAFF *and* BARDOLPH

FAL.   Bardolph, get thee before to Coventry; fill me a bottle of sack: our
soldiers shall march through; we'll to Sutton Co'fil'[1] to-night.
BARD.   Will you give me money, captain?
FAL.   Lay out, lay out.
BARD.   This bottle makes an angel.[2]
FAL.   An if it do, take it for thy labour; and if it make twenty, take them
all; I'll answer the coinage. Bid my lieutenant Peto meet me at
town's end.
BARD.   I will, captain: farewell.   [*Exit.*
FAL.   If I be not ashamed of my soldiers, I am a soused gurnet.[3] I have
misused the king's press[4] damnably. I have got, in exchange of a
hundred and fifty soldiers, three hundred and odd pounds. I press
me none but good householders, yeomen's sons; inquire me out
contracted bachelors, such as had been asked twice on the banns;
such a commodity of warm slaves, as had as lieve hear the devil
as a drum; such as fear the report of a caliver[5] worse than a struck
fowl or a hurt wild-duck. I pressed me none but such toasts-and-
butter, with hearts in their bellies no bigger than pins'-heads, and
they have bought out their services; and now my whole charge
consists of ancients,[6] corporals, lieutenants, gentlemen of compa-

---

1. *Sutton Co'fil'*] Sutton Coldfield, some twenty-five miles northwest of Coventry.
2. *angel*] coin worth ten shillings.
3. *soused gurnet*] a pickled fish; a term of contempt.
4. *king's press*] the royal commission for impressing soldiers.
5. *caliver*] musket.
6. *ancients*] ensigns.

nies, slaves as ragged as Lazarus in the painted cloth,[7] where the
glutton's dogs licked his sores; and such as indeed were never soldiers, but discarded unjust serving-men, younger sons to younger
brothers, revolted tapsters, and ostlers trade-fallen; the cankers of a
calm world and a long peace, ten times more dishonourable ragged than an old faced ancient: and such have I, to fill up the rooms
of them that have bought out their services, that you would think
that I had a hundred and fifty tattered prodigals lately come from
swine-keeping, from eating draff[8] and husks. A mad fellow met me
on the way and told me I had unloaded all the gibbets[9] and pressed
the dead bodies. No eye hath seen such scarecrows. I'll not march
through Coventry with them, that's flat: nay, and the villains march
wide betwixt the legs, as if they had gyves[10] on; for indeed I had
the most of them out of prison. There's but a shirt and a half in all
my company; and the half shirt is two napkins tacked together and
thrown over the shoulders like a herald's coat without sleeves; and
the shirt, to say the truth, stolen from my host at Saint Alban's, or
the red-nose innkeeper of Daventry.[11] But that's all one; they'll find
linen enough on every hedge.

Enter the PRINCE and WESTMORELAND

PRINCE. How now, blown Jack! how now, quilt!
FAL. What, Hal! how now, mad wag! what a devil dost thou in
Warwickshire? My good Lord of Westmoreland, I cry you mercy: I
thought your honour had already been at Shrewsbury.
WEST. Faith, Sir John, 'tis more than time that I were there, and you
too; but my powers are there already. The king, I can tell you, looks
for us all: we must away all night.
FAL. Tut, never fear me: I am as vigilant as a cat to steal cream.
PRINCE. I think, to steal cream indeed, for thy theft hath already made
thee butter. But tell me, Jack, whose fellows are these that come
after?
FAL. Mine, Hal, mine.
PRINCE. I did never see such pitiful rascals.
FAL. Tut, tut; good enough to toss;[12] food for powder, food for powder;
they'll fill a pit as well as better: tush, man, mortal men, mortal
men.

---

7. *Lazarus in the painted cloth*] The story of Lazarus and other scriptural tales were often
   depicted in the painted cloths or rough tapestries which adorned middle-class houses.
8. *draff*] refuse.
9. *gibbets*] gallows.
10. *gyves*] shackles, fetters.
11. *Saint Alban's . . . Daventry*] towns on the direct road from London to Coventry.
12. *to toss*] i.e., on a pike.

WEST.　Ay, but, Sir John, methinks they are exceeding poor and bare, too beggarly.
FAL.　Faith, for their poverty, I know not where they had that; and for their bareness, I am sure they never learned that of me.
PRINCE.　No, I'll be sworn; unless you call three fingers on the ribs[13] bare. But, sirrah, make haste: Percy is already in the field.
FAL.　What, is the king encamped?
WEST.　He is, Sir John: I fear we shall stay too long.
FAL.　Well,
　　　To the latter end of a fray and the beginning of a feast
　　　Fits a dull fighter and a keen guest.　　　　　　　*[Exeunt.*

SCENE III.　*The Rebel Camp near Shrewsbury.*

Enter HOTSPUR, WORCESTER, DOUGLAS, *and* VERNON

HOT.　We'll fight with him to-night.
WOR.　　　　　　　　　　　　　It may not be.
DOUG.　You give him then advantage.
VER.　　　　　　　　　　　　　Not a whit.
HOT.　Why say you so? looks he not for supply?
VER.　So do we.
HOT.　　　　　　His is certain, ours is doubtful.
WOR.　Good cousin, be advised; stir not to-night.
VER.　Do not, my lord.
DOUG.　　　　　　　You do not counsel well:
　　　You speak it out of fear and cold heart.
VER.　Do me no slander, Douglas: by my life,
　　　And I dare well maintain it with my life,
　　　If well-respected honour bid me on,
　　　I hold as little counsel with weak fear
　　　As you, my lord, or any Scot that this day lives:
　　　Let it be seen to-morrow in the battle
　　　Which of us fears.
DOUG.　　　　　　Yea, or to-night.
VER.　　　　　　　　　　　　　Content.
HOT.　To-night, say I.
VER.　Come, come, it may not be. I wonder much,

---

13. *three fingers . . . ribs]* three fingers' breadth of flesh.

Being men of such great leading as you are,
That you foresee not what impediments
Drag back our expedition: certain horse
Of my cousin Vernon's are not yet come up:
Your uncle Worcester's horse came but to-day;
And now their pride and mettle is asleep,
Their courage with hard labour tame and dull,
That not a horse is half the half of himself.

HOT.   So are the horses of the enemy
In general, journey-bated[1] and brought low:
The better part of ours are full of rest.

WOR.   The number of the king exceedeth ours:
For God's sake, cousin, stay till all come in.

                    [*The trumpet sounds a parley.*

Enter SIR WALTER BLUNT

BLUNT.   I come with gracious offers from the king,
If you vouchsafe me hearing and respect.

HOT.   Welcome, Sir Walter Blunt; and would to God
You were of our determination!
Some of us love you well; and even those some
Envy your great deservings and good name,
Because you are not of our quality,
But stand against us like an enemy.

BLUNT.   And God defend but still I should stand so,
So long as out of limit and true rule
You stand against anointed majesty.
But to my charge. The king hath sent to know
The nature of your griefs, and whereupon
You conjure from the breast of civil peace
Such bold hostility, teaching his duteous land
Audacious cruelty. If that the king
Have any way your good deserts forgot,
Which he confesseth to be manifold,
He bids you name your griefs; and with all speed
You shall have your desires with interest,
And pardon absolute for yourself and these
Herein misled by your suggestion.[2]

HOT.   The king is kind; and well we know the king
Knows at what time to promise, when to pay.
My father and my uncle and myself

---

1. *journey-bated*] exhausted with travel.
2. *by your suggestion*] at your prompting, instigation.

Did give him that same royalty he wears;
And when he was not six and twenty strong,
Sick in the world's regard, wretched and low,
A poor unminded outlaw sneaking home,
My father gave him welcome to the shore;
And when he heard him swear and vow to God
He came but to be Duke of Lancaster,
To sue his livery[3] and beg his peace,
With tears of innocency and terms of zeal,
My father, in kind heart and pity moved,
Swore him assistance and perform'd it too.
Now when the lords and barons of the realm
Perceived Northumberland did lean to him,
The more and less came in with cap and knee;
Met him in boroughs, cities, villages,
Attended him on bridges, stood in lanes,
Laid gifts before him, proffer'd him their oaths,
Gave him their heirs, as pages follow'd him
Even at the heels in golden multitudes.
He presently, as greatness knows itself,
Steps me a little higher than his vow
Made to my father, while his blood was poor,[4]
Upon the naked shore of Ravenspurgh;
And now, forsooth, takes on him to reform
Some certain edicts and some strait decrees
That lie too heavy on the commonwealth,
Cries out upon abuses, seems to weep
Over his country's wrongs; and by this face,
This seeming brow of justice, did he win
The hearts of all that he did angle for;
Proceeded further; cut me off the heads
Of all the favourites that the absent king
In deputation left behind him here,
When he was personal[5] in the Irish war.

BLUNT.   Tut, I came not to hear this.
HOT.   Then to the point.
In short time after, he deposed the king;
Soon after that, deprived him of his life;
And in the neck of that,[6] task'd the whole state;

---

3. *sue his livery*] sue for the return of his lands.
4. *while his blood was poor*] while he was in poor, dispirited condition.
5. *was personal*] was present in person.
6. *in the neck of that*] following quick on that.

To make that worse, suffer'd his kinsman March,
Who is, if every owner were well placed,
Indeed his king, to be engaged[7] in Wales,
There without ransom to lie forfeited;
Disgraced me in my happy victories,
Sought to entrap me by intelligence;[8]
Rated mine uncle from the council-board;
In rage dismiss'd my father from the court;
Broke oath on oath, committed wrong on wrong,
And in conclusion drove us to seek out
This head of safety,[9] and withal to pry
Into his title, the which we find
Too indirect for long continuance.
BLUNT.   Shall I return this answer to the king?
HOT.   Not so, Sir Walter: we'll withdraw a while.
Go to the king; and let there be impawn'd
Some surety for a safe return again,
And in the morning early shall mine uncle
Bring him our purposes: and so farewell.
BLUNT.   I would you would accept of grace and love.
HOT.   And may be so we shall.
BLUNT.   Pray God you do.   [*Exeunt.*

SCENE IV.   *York. The Archbishop's Palace.*

Enter the ARCHBISHOP OF YORK *and* SIR MICHAEL

ARCH.   Hie, good Sir Michael; bear this sealed brief[1]
With winged haste to the lord marshal;
This to my cousin Scroop, and all the rest
To whom they are directed. If you knew
How much they do import, you would make haste.
SIR M.   My good lord,
I guess their tenour.

---

7. *engaged*] pledged as a hostage.
8. *by intelligence*] by means of spies.
9. *head of safety*] armed force for our self-protection.

---

1. *brief*] letter.

ARCH.   Like enough you do.
     To-morrow, good Sir Michael, is a day
     Wherein the fortune of ten thousand men
     Must bide the touch;[2] for, sir, at Shrewsbury,
     As I am truly given to understand,
     The king with mighty and quick-raised power
     Meets with Lord Harry: and, I fear, Sir Michael,
     What with the sickness of Northumberland,
     Whose power was in the first proportion,
     And what with Owen Glendower's absence thence,
     Who with them was a rated sinew[3] too
     And comes not in, o'er-ruled by prophecies,
     I fear the power of Percy is too weak
     To wage an instant trial with the king.
SIR M.   Why, my good lord, you need not fear;
     There is Douglas and Lord Mortimer.
ARCH.   No, Mortimer is not there.
SIR M.   But there is Mordake, Vernon, Lord Harry Percy,
     And there is my Lord of Worcester and a head
     Of gallant warriors, noble gentlemen.
ARCH.   And so there is: but yet the king hath drawn
     The special head of all the land together:
     The Prince of Wales, Lord John of Lancaster,
     The noble Westmoreland and warlike Blunt;
     And many mo corrivals[4] and dear men
     Of estimation and command in arms.
SIR M.   Doubt not, my lord, they shall be well opposed.
ARCH.   I hope no less, yet needful 'tis to fear;
     And, to prevent the worst, Sir Michael, speed:
     For if Lord Percy thrive not, ere the king
     Dismiss his power, he means to visit us,
     For he hath heard of our confederacy,
     And 'tis but wisdom to make strong against him:
     Therefore make haste. I must go write again
     To other friends; and so farewell, Sir Michael.   [*Exeunt.*

---

2. *bide the touch*] stand the test.
3. *a rated sinew*] an anticipated source of strength.
4. *mo corrivals*] more partners in the enterprise.

ACT V

SCENE I. *The King's Camp near Shrewsbury.*

Enter the KING, PRINCE OF WALES, LORD JOHN OF LANCASTER,
SIR WALTER BLUNT, *and* FALSTAFF

KING.   How bloodily the sun begins to peer
Above yon busky[1] hill! the day looks pale
At his distemperature.[2]
PRINCE.   The southern wind
Doth play the trumpet to his purposes,
And by his hollow whistling in the leaves
Foretells a tempest and a blustering day.
KING.   Then with the losers let it sympathise,
For nothing can seem foul to those that win. [*The trumpet sounds.*

Enter WORCESTER *and* VERNON

How now, my Lord of Worcester! 'tis not well
That you and I should meet upon such terms
As now we meet. You have deceived our trust,
And made us doff our easy robes of peace.
To crush our old limbs in ungentle steel:
This is not well, my lord, this is not well.
What say you to it? will you again unknit
This churlish knot of all-abhorred war?
And move in that obedient orb[3] again
Where you did give a fair and natural light,
And be no more an exhaled meteor,[4]

---

1. *busky*] bushy, wooded.
2. *distemperature*] inclemency.
3. *obedient orb*] orbit of obedience.
4. *an exhaled meteor*] meteors were supposed to be formed of vapours drawn out of the earth
by the sun, and were regarded as ill omens.

71

A prodigy of fear, and a portent
Of broached mischief to the unborn times?
WOR.   Hear me, my liege:
For mine own part, I could be well content
To entertain the lag-end of my life
With quiet hours; for, I do protest
I have not sought the day of this dislike.
KING.   You have not sought it! how comes it, then?
FAL.   Rebellion lay in his way, and he found it.
PRINCE.   Peace, chewet,[5] peace!
WOR.   It pleased your majesty to turn your looks
Of favour from myself and all our house;
And yet I must remember you,[6] my lord,
We were the first and dearest of your friends.
For you my staff of office did I break
In Richard's time; and posted day and night
To meet you on the way, and kiss your hand,
When yet you were in place and in account
Nothing so strong and fortunate as I.
It was myself, my brother, and his son,
That brought you home, and boldly did outdare
The dangers of the time. You swore to us,
And you did swear that oath at Doncaster,
That you did nothing purpose 'gainst the state;
Nor claim no further than your new-fall'n right,
The seat of Gaunt, dukedom of Lancaster:
To this we swore our aid. But in short space
It rain'd down fortune showering on your head;
And such a flood of greatness fell on you,
What with our help, what with the absent king,
What with the injuries of a wanton time,
The seeming sufferances[7] that you had borne,
And the contrarious winds that held the king
So long in his unlucky Irish wars
That all in England did repute him dead;
And from this swarm of fair advantages
You took occasion to be quickly woo'd
To gripe the general sway into your hand;
Forgot your oath to us at Doncaster;
And being fed by us you used us so

5. *chewet*] a kind of pie, made of minced meat.
6. *remember you*] remind you.
7. *sufferances*] sufferings.

As that ungentle gull, the cuckoo's bird,
Useth the sparrow;[8] did oppress our nest;
Grew by our feeding to so great a bulk
That even our love durst not come near your sight
For fear of swallowing; but with nimble wing
We were enforced, for safety sake, to fly
Out of your sight and raise this present head;
Whereby we stand opposed by such means
As you yourself have forged against yourself,
By unkind usage, dangerous countenance,
And violation of all faith and troth
Sworn to us in your younger enterprise.

KING.   These things indeed you have articulate,[9]
Proclaim'd at market-crosses, read in churches,
To face[10] the garment of rebellion
With some fine colour that may please the eye
Of fickle changelings and poor discontents,
Which gape and rub the elbow[11] at the news
Of hurlyburly innovation:
And never yet did insurrection want
Such water-colours to impaint his cause;
Nor moody beggars, starving for a time
Of pellmell havoc and confusion.

PRINCE.   In both your armies there is many a soul
Shall pay full dearly for this encounter,
If once they join in trial. Tell your nephew,
The Prince of Wales doth join with all the world
In praise of Henry Percy: by my hopes,
This present enterprise set off his head,[12]
I do not think a braver gentleman,
More active-valiant or more valiant-young,
More daring or more bold, is now alive
To grace this latter age with noble deeds.
For my part, I may speak it to my shame,
I have a truant been to chivalry;
And so I hear he doth account me too;
Yet this before my father's majesty —
I am content that he shall take the odds

---

8. *cuckoo's bird . . . sparrow*] the cuckoo was thought to lay its eggs in the sparrow's nest, and the young cuckoo would eat its host as soon as it was old enough.
9. *articulate*] set out in articles, formally defined.
10. *face*] trim, give plausible edge to.
11. *rub the elbow*] a gesture of satisfaction.
12. *set off his head*] struck off his record.

Of his great name and estimation,
And will, to save the blood on either side,
Try fortune with him in a single fight.

KING. And, Prince of Wales, so dare we venture thee,
Albeit considerations infinite
Do make against it. No, good Worcester, no,
We love our people well; even those we love
That are misled upon your cousin's part;
And, will they take the offer of our grace,
Both he and they and you, yea, every man
Shall be my friend again and I'll be his:
So tell your cousin, and bring me word
What he will do: but if he will not yield,
Rebuke and dread correction wait on us
And they shall do their office. So, be gone;
We will not now be troubled with reply:
We offer fair; take it advisedly.   [*Exeunt Worcester and Vernon.*

PRINCE. It will not be accepted, on my life:
The Douglas and the Hotspur both together
Are confident against the world in arms.

KING. Hence, therefore, every leader to his charge;
For, on their answer, will we set on them:
And God befriend us, as our cause is just!
                [*Exeunt all but the Prince of Wales and Falstaff.*

FAL. Hal, if thou see me down in the battle, and bestride me, so; 'tis a
point of friendship.

PRINCE. Nothing but a colossus can do thee that friendship. Say thy
prayers, and farewell.

FAL. I would 'twere bed-time, Hal, and all well.

PRINCE. Why, thou owest God a death.   [*Exit.*

FAL. 'Tis not due yet; I would be loath to pay him before his day. What
need I be so forward with him that calls not on me? Well, 'tis no
matter; honour pricks me on. Yea, but how if honour prick me off
when I come on? how then? Can honour set to a leg? no: or an
arm? no: or take away the grief of a wound? no. Honour hath no
skill in surgery, then? no. What is honour? a word. What is in that
word honour? what is that honour? air. A trim reckoning! Who
hath it? he that died o' Wednesday. Doth he feel it? no. Doth he
hear it? no. 'Tis insensible, then? yea, to the dead. But will it not
live with the living? no. Why? detraction will not suffer it. Therefore I'll none of it. Honour is a mere scutcheon:[13] and so ends my
catechism.   [*Exit.*

---

13. *a mere scutcheon*] mere heraldic blazonry.

SCENE II. *The Rebel Camp.*

Enter WORCESTER *and* VERNON

WOR.   O, no, my nephew must not know, Sir Richard,
    The liberal and kind offer of the king.
VER.   'T were best he did.
WOR.   Then are we all undone.
    It is not possible, it cannot be,
    The king should keep his word in loving us;
    He will suspect us still, and find a time
    To punish this offence in other faults:
    Suspicion all our lives shall be stuck full of eyes;
    For treason is but trusted like the fox,
    Who, ne'er so tame, so cherish'd and lock'd up,
    Will have a wild trick of his ancestors.
    Look how we can, or sad or merrily,
    Interpretation will misquote[1] our looks,
    And we shall feed like oxen at a stall,
    The better cherish'd, still the nearer death.
    My nephew's trespass may be well forgot;
    It hath the excuse of youth and heat of blood;
    And an adopted name of privilege,
    A hare-brain'd Hotspur,[2] govern'd by a spleen:
    All his offences live upon my head
    And on his father's; we did train him on,
    And, his corruption being ta'en from us,
    We, as the spring of all, shall pay for all.
    Therefore, good cousin, let not Harry know,
    In any case, the offer of the king.
VER.   Deliver what you will; I'll say 'tis so.
    Here comes your cousin.

Enter HOTSPUR *and* DOUGLAS

HOT.   My uncle is return'd:
    Deliver up my Lord of Westmoreland.
    Uncle, what news?

---

1. *misquote*] misread, misunderstand.
2. *an adopted . . . Hotspur*] the assumed name of Hotspur may serve to justify his rash acts.

WOR.   The king will bid you battle presently.
DOUG.   Defy him by the Lord of Westmoreland.
HOT.   Lord Douglas, go you and tell him so.
DOUG.   Marry, and shall, and very willingly.   [*Exit.*
WOR.   There is no seeming mercy in the king.
HOT.   Did you beg any? God forbid!
WOR.   I told him gently of our grievances,
          Of his oath-breaking; which he mended thus,
          By now forswearing that he is forsworn:
          He calls us rebels, traitors; and will scourge
          With haughty arms this hateful name in us.

Re-enter DOUGLAS

DOUG.   Arm, gentlemen; to arms! for I have thrown
          A brave defiance in King Henry's teeth,
          And Westmoreland, that was engaged, did bear it;
          Which cannot choose but bring him quickly on.
WOR.   The Prince of Wales stepp'd forth before the king,
          And, nephew, challenged you to single fight.
HOT.   O, would the quarrel lay upon our heads,
          And that no man might draw short breath to-day
          But I and Harry Monmouth! Tell me, tell me,
          How show'd his tasking?[3] seem'd it in contempt?
VER.   No, by my soul; I never in my life
          Did hear a challenge urged more modestly,
          Unless a brother should a brother dare
          To gentle exercise and proof of arms.
          He gave you all the duties of a man;
          Trimm'd up your praises with a princely tongue,
          Spoke your deservings like a chronicle,
          Making you ever better than his praise
          By still dispraising praise valued with you;
          And, which became him like a prince indeed,
          He made a blushing cital[4] of himself;
          And chid his truant youth with such a grace
          As if he master'd there a double spirit
          Of teaching and of learning instantly.
          There did he pause: but let me tell the world,
          If he outlive the envy of this day,
          England did never owe so sweet a hope,
          So much misconstrued in his wantonness.

---

3. *tasking*] challenge.
4. *cital*] impeachment.

HOT. Cousin, I think thou art enamoured
    On his follies: never did I hear
    Of any prince so wild a libertine.
    But be he as he will, yet once ere night
    I will embrace him with a soldier's arm,
    That he shall shrink under my courtesy.
    Arm, arm with speed: and, fellows, soldiers, friends,
    Better consider what you have to do
    Than I, that have not well the gift of tongue,
    Can lift your blood up with persuasion.

Enter a Messenger

MESS. My lord, here are letters for you.
HOT. I cannot read them now.
    O gentlemen, the time of life is short!
    To spend that shortness basely were too long,
    If life did ride upon a dial's point,
    Still ending at the arrival of an hour.
    An if we live, we live to tread on kings;
    If die, brave death, when princes die with us!
    Now, for our consciences, the arms are fair,
    When the intent of bearing them is just.

Enter another Messenger

MESS. My lord, prepare; the king comes on apace.
HOT. I thank him, that he cuts me from my tale,
    For I profess not talking; only this —
    Let each man do his best: and here draw I
    A sword, whose temper I intend to stain
    With the best blood that I can meet withal
    In the adventure of this perilous day.
    Now, Esperance! Percy! and set on.
    Sound all the lofty instruments of war,
    And by that music let us all embrace;
    For, heaven to earth, some of us never shall
    A second time do such a courtesy.
               [*The trumpets sound. They embrace and exeunt.*

SCENE III. *Plain between the Camps.*

The King enters with his power. Alarum to the battle. Then enter
DOUGLAS *and* SIR WALTER BLUNT

BLUNT.   What is thy name, that in the battle thus
  Thou crossest me? what honour dost thou seek
  Upon my head?
DOUG.   Know then, my name is Douglas;
  And I do haunt thee in the battle thus,
  Because some tell me that thou art a king.
BLUNT.   They tell thee true.
DOUG.   The Lord of Stafford dear to-day hath bought
  Thy likeness; for instead of thee, King Harry,
  This sword hath ended him: so shall it thee,
  Unless thou yield thee as my prisoner.
BLUNT.   I was not born a yielder, thou proud Scot;
  And thou shalt find a king that will revenge
  Lord Stafford's death.   [*They fight. Douglas kills Blunt.*

Enter HOTSPUR

HOT.   O Douglas, hadst thou fought at Holmedon thus,
  I never had triumph'd upon a Scot.
DOUG.   All's done, all's won; here breathless lies the king.
HOT.   Where?
DOUG.   Here.
HOT.   This, Douglas? no: I know this face full well:
  A gallant knight he was, his name was Blunt;
  Semblably furnish'd[1] like the king himself.
DOUG.   A fool go with thy soul, whither it goes!
  A borrowed title hast thou bought too dear:
  Why didst thou tell me that thou wert a king?
HOT.   The king hath many marching in his coats.
DOUG.   Now, by my sword, I will kill all his coats;
  I'll murder all his wardrobe, piece by piece,
  Until I meet the king.
HOT.   Up, and away!
  Our soldiers stand full fairly for the day.   [*Exeunt.*

---

1. *Semblably furnish'd*] Similarly equipped.

Alarum. Enter FALSTAFF, *solus*

FAL. Though I could 'scape shot-free² at London, I fear the shot here;
here's no scoring³ but upon the pate. Soft! who are you? Sir Walter
Blunt: there's honour for you! here's no vanity! I am as hot as molten
lead, and as heavy too: God keep lead out of me! I need no more
weight than mine own bowels. I have led my ragamuffins where
they are peppered: there's not three of my hundred and fifty left
alive; and they are for the town's end, to beg during life. But who
comes here?

Enter the PRINCE

PRINCE. What, stand'st thou idle here? lend me thy sword:
    Many a nobleman lies stark and stiff
    Under the hoofs of vaunting enemies,
    Whose deaths are yet unrevenged: I prithee, lend me thy sword.
FAL. O Hal, I prithee, give me leave to breathe a while. Turk Gregory⁴
never did such deeds in arms as I have done this day. I have paid
Percy, I have made him sure.
PRINCE. He is, indeed; and living to kill thee. I prithee, lend me thy
sword.
FAL. Nay, before God, Hal, if Percy be alive, thou get'st not my sword;
but take my pistol, if thou wilt.
PRINCE. Give it me: what, is it in the case?
FAL. Ay, Hal; 'tis hot, 'tis hot; there's that will sack a city.
                    [*The Prince draws it out, and finds it to be a bottle of sack.*
PRINCE. What, is it a time to jest and dally now?
                                    [*He throws the bottle at him. Exit.*
FAL. Well, if Percy be alive, I'll pierce him. If he do come in my way, so:
if he do not, if I come in his willingly, let him make a carbonado⁵
of me. I like not such grinning honour as Sir Walter hath: give me
life: which if I can save, so; if not, honour comes unlooked for, and
there's an end.   [*Exit.*

---

2. *shot-free*] without paying the bill.
3. *scoring*] marking up of charges.
4. *Turk Gregory*] A reference to the militant pope Gregory VII.
5. *carbonado*] piece of meat slashed for broiling.

SCENE IV. *Another Part of the Field.*

Alarum. Excursions. Enter the KING, *the* PRINCE, LORD JOHN OF
LANCASTER, *and* EARL OF WESTMORELAND

KING.   I prithee,
    Harry, withdraw thyself; thou bleed'st too much.
    Lord John of Lancaster, go you with him.
LAN.   Not I, my lord, unless I did bleed too.
PRINCE.   I beseech your majesty, make up,[1]
    Lest your retirement do amaze[2] your friends.
KING.   I will do so.
    My Lord of Westmoreland, lead him to his tent.
WEST.   Come, my lord, I'll lead you to your tent.
PRINCE.   Lead me, my lord? I do not need your help:
    And God forbid a shallow scratch should drive
    The Prince of Wales from such a field as this,
    Where stain'd nobility lies trodden on,
    And rebels' arms triumph in massacres!
LAN.   We breathe too long: come, cousin Westmoreland,
    Our duty this way lies; for God's sake, come.
                [Exeunt Prince John and Westmoreland.
PRINCE.   By God, thou hast deceived me, Lancaster;
    I did not think thee lord of such a spirit:
    Before, I loved thee as a brother, John;
    But now, I do respect thee as my soul.
KING.   I saw him hold Lord Percy at the point,[3]
    With lustier maintenance than I did look for
    Of such an ungrown warrior.
PRINCE.   O, this boy
    Lends mettle to us all!   *[Exit.*

Enter DOUGLAS

DOUG.   Another king! they grow like Hydra's heads:
    I am the Douglas, fatal to all those
    That wear those colours on them: what art thou,
    That counterfeit'st the person of a king?
KING.   The king himself; who, Douglas, grieves at heart
    So many of his shadows thou hast met

1. *make up*] advance.
2. *amaze*] bewilder, strike with panic.
3. *hold Lord Percy at the point*] parry Lord Percy's blows.

And not the very king. I have two boys
Seek Percy and thyself about the field:
But, seeing thou fall'st on me so luckily,
I will assay thee: so, defend thyself.
DOUG.   I fear thou art another counterfeit;
And yet, in faith, thou bear'st thee like a king:
But mine I am sure thou art, whoe'er thou be,
And thus I win thee.   [*They fight; the King being in danger,*
re-enter Prince of Wales.
PRINCE.   Hold up thy head, vile Scot, or thou art like
Never to hold it up again! the spirits
Of valiant Shirley, Stafford, Blunt, are in my arms:
It is the Prince of Wales that threatens thee;
Who never promiseth but he means to pay.
        [*They fight: Douglas flies.*
Cheerly, my lord; how fares your grace?
Sir Nicholas Gawsey hath for succour sent,
And so hath Clifton: I'll to Clifton straight.
KING.   Stay, and breathe a while:
Thou hast redeem'd thy lost opinion,
And show'd thou makest some tender of[4] my life,
In this fair rescue thou hast brought to me.
PRINCE.   O God! they did me too much injury
That ever said I hearken'd for[5] your death.
If it were so, I might have let alone
The insulting hand of Douglas over you,
Which would have been as speedy in your end
As all the poisonous potions in the world,
And saved the treacherous labour of your son.
KING.   Make up to Clifton: I'll to Sir Nicholas Gawsey.   [*Exit.*

Enter HOTSPUR

HOT.   If I mistake not, thou art Harry Monmouth.
PRINCE.   Thou speak'st as if I would deny my name.
HOT.   My name is Harry Percy.
PRINCE.   Why, then I see
A very valiant rebel of the name.
I am the Prince of Wales; and think not, Percy,
To share with me in glory any more:
Two stars keep not their motion in one sphere;
Nor can one England brook a double reign,

---

4. *makest some tender of*] showest some regard for.
5. *hearken'd for*] waited for.

Of Harry Percy and the Prince of Wales.
HOT.   Nor shall it, Harry; for the hour is come
       To end the one of us; and would to God
       Thy name in arms were now as great as mine!
PRINCE.   I'll make it greater ere I part from thee;
       And all the budding honours on thy crest
       I'll crop, to make a garland for my head.
HOT.   I can no longer brook thy vanities.   [*They fight.*

Enter FALSTAFF

FAL.   Well said, Hal! to it, Hal! Nay, you shall find no boy's play here, I
       can tell you.

Re-enter DOUGLAS; *he fights with* FALSTAFF, *who falls down as if he
were dead, and exit* DOUGLAS. HOTSPUR *is wounded, and falls*

HOT.   O, Harry, thou hast robb'd me of my youth!
       I better brook the loss of brittle life
       Than those proud titles thou hast won of me;
       They wound my thoughts worse than thy sword my flesh:
       But thought's the slave of life, and life time's fool;
       And time, that takes survey of all the world,
       Must have a stop.[6] O, I could prophesy,
       But that the earthy and cold hand of death
       Lies on my tongue: no, Percy, thou art dust,
       And food for —   [*Dies.*
PRINCE.   For worms, brave Percy: fare thee well, great heart!
       Ill-weaved ambition, how much art thou shrunk!
       When that this body did contain a spirit,
       A kingdom for it was too small a bound;
       But now two paces of the vilest earth
       Is room enough: this earth that bears thee dead
       Bears not alive so stout a gentleman.
       If thou wert sensible of courtesy,
       I should not make so dear a show of zeal:
       But let my favours[7] hide thy mangled face;
       And, even in thy behalf, I'll thank myself
       For doing these fair rites of tenderness.
       Adieu, and take thy praise with thee to heaven!
       Thy ignominy sleep with thee in the grave,
       But not remember'd in thy epitaph!
                      [*He spieth Falstaff on the ground.*

---

6. *thought's . . . stop*] thought depends on life; life obeys the caprice of time, and time, that
   embraces all the world in its sway, must have an end.
7. *favours*] ribbons worn as a scarf.

What, old acquaintance! could not all this flesh
Keep in a little life? Poor Jack, farewell!
I could have better spared a better man:
O, I should have a heavy miss of thee,
If I were much in love with vanity!
Death hath not struck so fat a deer to-day,
Though many dearer, in this bloody fray.
Embowell'd[8] will I see thee by and by:
Till then in blood by noble Percy lie.   [*Exit.*

FAL. [*Rising up*] Embowelled! if thou embowel me to-day, I'll give you leave to powder[9] me and eat me too to-morrow. 'Sblood, 'twas time to counterfeit, or that hot termagant Scot had paid me scot and lot[10] too. Counterfeit? I lie, I am no counterfeit: to die, is to be a counterfeit; for he is but the counterfeit of a man who hath not the life of a man: but to counterfeit dying, when a man thereby liveth, is to be no counterfeit, but the true and perfect image of life indeed. The better part of valour is discretion; in the which better part I have saved my life. 'Zounds, I am afraid of this gunpowder Percy, though he be dead: how, if he should counterfeit too, and rise? by my faith, I am afraid he would prove the better counterfeit. Therefore I'll make him sure; yea, and I'll swear I killed him. Why may he not rise as well as I? Nothing confutes me but eyes, and nobody sees me. Therefore, sirrah [*stabbing him*], with a new wound in your thigh, come you along with me.

                          [*Takes up Hotspur on his back.*

Re-enter the PRINCE OF WALES *and* LORD JOHN OF LANCASTER

PRINCE. Come, brother John; full bravely hast thou flesh'd[11]
          Thy maiden sword.
LAN.   But, soft! whom have we here?
          Did you not tell me this fat man was dead?
PRINCE. I did; I saw him dead,
          Breathless and bleeding on the ground. Art thou alive?
          Or is it fantasy that plays upon our eyesight?
          I prithee, speak; we will not trust our eyes
          Without our ears: thou art not what thou seem'st.
FAL. No, that's certain; I am not a double man: but if I be not Jack Falstaff, then am I a Jack.[12] There is Percy [*throwing the body*

---

8. *Embowell'd*] Embowelled for burial.
9. *powder*] pickle or salt.
10. *scot and lot*] used figuratively to denote complete payment.
11. *fleshed*] initiated.
12. *a Jack*] a Jackanapes.

down]: if your father will do me any honour, so; if not, let him
kill the next Percy himself. I look to be either earl or duke, I can
assure you.

PRINCE.   Why, Percy I killed myself, and saw thee dead.

FAL.   Didst thou? Lord, Lord, how this world is given to lying! I grant
you I was down and out of breath; and so was he: but we rose both
at an instant, and fought a long hour by Shrewsbury clock. If I may
be believed, so; if not, let them that should reward valour bear the
sin upon their own heads. I'll take it upon my death,[13] I gave him
this wound in the thigh: if the man were alive, and would deny it,
'zounds, I would make him eat a piece of my sword.

LAN.   This is the strangest tale that ever I heard.

PRINCE.   This is the strangest fellow, brother John.
     Come, bring your luggage nobly on your back:
     For my part, if a lie may do thee grace,
     I'll gild it with the happiest terms I have.   [*A retreat is sounded.*
     The trumpet sounds retreat; the day is ours.
     Come, brother, let us to the highest of the field,
     To see what friends are living, who are dead.
                          [*Exeunt Prince of Wales and Lancaster.*

FAL.   I'll follow, as they say, for reward. He that rewards me, God reward
him! If I do grow great, I'll grow less; for I'll purge, and leave sack,
and live cleanly as a nobleman should do.   [*Exit.*

SCENE V.   *Another Part of the Field.*

The trumpets sound. Enter the KING, PRINCE OF WALES,
LORD JOHN OF LANCASTER, EARL OF WESTMORELAND,
with WORCESTER *and* VERNON *prisoners*

KING.   Thus ever did rebellion find rebuke.
     Ill-spirited[1] Worcester! did not we send grace,
     Pardon and terms of love to all of you?
     And wouldst thou turn our offers contrary?
     Misuse the tenour of thy kinsman's trust?
     Three knights upon our party slain to-day,

---

13.   *I'll take it upon my death*] I'll stake my life on it.

---

1.   *Ill-spirited*] Of evil disposition.

A noble earl and many a creature else
Had been alive this hour,
If like a Christian thou hadst truly borne
Betwixt our armies true intelligence.

WOR. What I have done my safety urged me to;
And I embrace this fortune patiently,
Since not to be avoided it falls on me.

KING. Bear Worcester to the death, and Vernon too:
Other offenders we will pause upon.

[*Exeunt Worcester and Vernon, guarded.*

How goes the field?

PRINCE. The noble Scot, Lord Douglas, when he saw
The fortune of the day quite turn'd from him,
The noble Percy slain, and all his men
Upon the foot of fear,[2] fled with the rest;
And falling from a hill, he was so bruised
That the pursuers took him. At my tent
The Douglas is; and I beseech your grace
I may dispose of him.

KING. With all my heart.

PRINCE. Then, brother John of Lancaster, to you
This honourable bounty shall belong:
Go to the Douglas, and deliver him
Up to his pleasure, ransomless and free:
His valour shown upon our crests to-day
Hath taught us how to cherish such high deeds
Even in the bosom of our adversaries.

LAN. I thank your grace for this high courtesy,
Which I shall give away immediately.

KING. Then this remains, that we divide our power.
You, son John, and my cousin Westmoreland
Towards York shall bend you with your dearest speed,[3]
To meet Northumberland and the prelate Scroop,
Who, as we hear, are busily in arms:
Myself and you, son Harry, will towards Wales,
To fight with Glendower and the Earl of March.
Rebellion in this land shall lose his sway,
Meeting the check of such another day:
And since this business so fair is done,
Let us not leave till all our own be won.

[*Exeunt.*

---

2. *Upon the foot of fear*] Rushing off in fear.
3. *the devil . . . fiddlestick*] a proverbial phrase; meaning, here's a to-do about nothing.